Baptism b

A Rick and Dante Paranormal Mystery

Mystery

By

Alexandra Gilchrist

Prologue

Revolutionary France 1793

Dante Brand tugged nervously at the finely embroidered white kid gloves he wore, the only reminder of his life in the French court only a few short months earlier. He'd packed away most of his more brightly colored *incroyable* clothes on the night Louis the Fourteenth was arrested – purely for survival – and now wore a cloak to cover one of his less flamboyant ensembles. Nothing could induce him to give up his gloves. White kid, lined with fiery orange silk, and embroidered with flaming phoenixes at his wrists. Designed by the King's own glover, they were the most expensive part of an already expensive wardrobe, and the piece he could least do without.

"By the Virgin, if you insist on wearing those things, at least keep them hidden inside your cloak sleeves." Friar Donadieu hissed. "The moonlight shines off them and you're going to get us all killed."

"Leave him be, Friar." Father Abreo laid a patient hand on the younger man's shoulder. "Dante has enough reason to wear the gloves, and I can assure you that there is little risk of him getting us killed."

Dante smiled at the priest thinly. Father Abreo was his confessor, and the only one other than King Louis himself that knew what he was. Louis had forbidden Dante from breaking him from the Tower. He didn't understand the order, but he would honor it. When the long and hideous fingers of the Revolution demanded all priests in the country swear allegiance to the State alone, he'd offered his services to Father Abreo instead. The priest also had refused to bend or to flee, citing care for his flock and lack of care for Madame Guillotine, so Dante had contented himself to be the avenging angel of the Church.

The day after nearly two hundred priests were drowned off Nantes, for no more of a crime than Father Abreo had committed, Dante had dug up his entire savings, and offered to ship Father Abreo and any of his parishioners who would leave to America. Other than clothes, Dante's needs had been few over the last 200 years, and the money was more than enough to bribe a trading vessel returning to America. In Revolutionary France, no one questioned where an aristo got his money, no matter the amount.

Tonight, November twenty-sixth, in the year of our Lord 1793, Dante kept a wary eye for dogs of the Committee. There was virtually no way for the escape of a wealthy aristo, companion to Louis himself, a refractory priest, and fifty peasants to avoid the notice of a nosy *sans culottes* looking to curry favor with the new government.

They were nearly in sight of the docks when he heard them, the high, mournful howl of Robespierre's hellhounds on the hunt.

Father Abreo looked at him with fearful eyes. "Hunting hounds, Dante?"

Dante gave him a reassuring smile and handed him a packet of papers. "I will deal with the hellhounds of the revolution. You make sure everyone gets aboard the *Franklin*."

"What if you..." Father Abreo lowered his voice. "How long should we wait?"

"Don't. I will catch up when I can." Dante had told the priest his secret, but things didn't always go as planned. He could catch another ship, his friends would only face increased danger if they stayed.

The otherworldly howl grew closer. It didn't sound like the dogs were between the refugees and the docks, so they were probably tracking from the direction they came. Dante picked an open intersection to make his stand. It was late, and few people roamed the streets. Lord willing, the rest would flee when the hellhounds arrived.

Dante took a deep breath and made the sign of the cross reverently. No priest he'd confessed to over the last two hundred years of his cursed existence had been able to tell him if a phoenix cursed to human form had an eternal soul, but all had been in agreement: as a creation of God, he owed whatever substance he did have to the service of his Creator. Dispatching the minions of darkness had always seemed an appropriate use of his gifts.

The chorus of howls were nearly upon him. With a sigh, he untied the strings of his cloak and cast it aside to reveal his carefully tailored green silk suit and delicately detailed orange satin waistcoat. If he had to fight, the cloak would be a burden; and if he had to die, he'd rather go out in glorious splendor.

Three hellhounds converged on his position. Each was easily as tall as Dante, with slick black fur and eyes that glowed red in the night. They came in low to the ground, snarling and baring teeth that were as long as his fingers. Teeth that would tear apart Father Abreo and the other refugees like a man would tear meat from a chicken leg. They had to end here, even if it meant Dante did as well.

He calmly pulled his hands free from his gloves and tucked the gloves into his waistband. As the hellhounds crept closer, he began to recite the Rosary, softly at first, then louder as they grew nearer. With a snarl, the center hound attacked. Dante spun aside gracefully like a bullfighter in Madrid, allowing both bare hands to comb through the hellhound's fur as it passed. The hellhound burst into flames at his touch and bounded away yelping and howling. The second pulled up short, frightened by his fellow's fate, but was already too close. Dante pressed his hands to the monstrous dog's flank, and it followed his leader.

The third hellhound caught him with a great swipe of his paw and sent him tumbling across the cobblestone road. Dante rolled to his hands and knees, wincing at the pain of at least one broken rib, but careful not to touch his hands to his own side. The suit was hand tailored by Louis' personal clothier, and he wouldn't get an opportunity to replace it quickly on the other side. He stood and scanned the intersection for the third hellhound. He'd lost track of it while fighting the other two, allowing it to get him down, a potentially fatal mistake.

Something sharp and vice-like grabbed him by the neck from behind. Fear spiked in the pit of his stomach in the split second he realized what had happened, then the hellhound bit down and shook, and everything went black.

Dante awoke thirty seconds later, in a smoldering ring of ash and to the sound of fae laughter. He'd died again. *Mince*, how he hated the disorientation that came with each resurrection! He shook his head and went through his mental checklist. Assess for a remaining threat. Usually whatever killed him was caught in the blast radius of his resurrection fire, but that didn't mean there weren't more. The charred skeleton of a hellhound lay on the borders of the scorched circle and no other threat seemed imminent. Second, find clothes. He swore more firmly this time as his memory slowly returned. That was an expensive suit, and all that he would be able to find here would be the tacky and plain *sans culottes* clothes of "good" revolutionary citizens. He was so disgusted at the thought of appearing before his friends in such clothes, that he strongly considered trying to catch another ship later when he could find more suitable clothes, but the corpse of the hellhound reminded him Father Abreo and the other refugees needed his protection until they were safely out of the reach of the Revolutionary Government.

With a sigh of resignation, Dante sifted his gloves and what coin had remained in his pocket from the ashes of his other clothes, pulled the gloves on over his hands, and headed for the nearest home. Even covered in soot, his finely embroidered kid gloves would mark him as a hated aristo, but it couldn't be helped. The gloves carried a special blessing that protected them from fire and kept him from burning everything he touched. Hopefully the disfigured gold coins would be enough to make up for his appearance.

"Get lost, drunken aristo, before I call the guard on you!" the citizen inside swore at him.

"I am not drunk, good citizen, but the hellhound destroyed my clothes." He held up the melted mass of coins. "I will pay for a complete outfit in gold."

With more cursing and colorful commentary on Dante's parentage and current condition, the peasant inside opened the door just enough to toss out a ragged set of clothes and a pair of boots with holes in the soles, and snatch the gold from Dante's hand before slamming it shut again.

Dante crouched next to the dirty pile and picked up a threadbare shirt sleeve by just a gloved thumb and forefinger. He was painfully aware that he was standing in the middle of a Parisian street wearing nothing but a pair of gloves, but the thought of putting those *rags* on seemed infinitely more embarrassing. He reminded himself that his trunk was already onboard the *Franklin*, so he only had to wear them long enough to get to the boat without getting arrested and sent to the guillotine. He swallowed his pride and pulled them on gingerly, the smell and the feeling of the course, dirty fabric against his skin nearly enough to bring him to tears.

He made it to the *Franklin* just as it was about to weigh anchor, to find Father Abreo at the gangplank watching for him. The priest gave his clothes a questioning look as he boarded.

"Don't ask." Dante brushed past him and headed for the hold. "Just tell the captain we're all aboard while I go find my own clothes again."

They cleared the harbor and made their way to the newly formed United States of America with no further issues, landing in New York over a month later. The captain and Father Abreo went ashore to try to organize entrance into the country for the shipload of refugees, a process that took far longer than Dante thought it should.

Surely they won't turn us away. Dante leaned on the ship's gunwale and looked out into the city. It was far smaller than Paris or London, with no palace or castle in sight. Ben Franklin had talked much about their new government when he had visited Paris in the years following the American's own revolution. He had explained it as something new and different, but frankly, having been in the service of the Crown of France for centuries left Dante with little concept of what that difference could possibly mean.

Dante stood up straighter. Father Abreo and the captain were returning, but they weren't alone. A trio of smartly dressed gentlemen in powdered wigs and fine coats followed behind. Their clothes weren't *Parisian* fine, but they looked as if they knew how to dress anyway. Perhaps these men could direct him to the President.

"Dante, these men specifically requested to see you," Father Abreo began as he boarded.

"Dante Brand, late in the service of King Louis the Fourteenth, at your service." Dante bowed deeply to the trio.

"Monsieur Brand, welcome to the United States of America." The lead man offered a tight-lipped smile and extended his hand. "I'm President George Washinton. Our mutual friend, Benjamin Franklin, told me a lot about you. We would love to extend you a place in our government similar to the one you held in France."

Chapter One

Patrick "Rick" McCoy sat down in a worn chair in the anteroom outside his boss's office. He had been looking forward to this meeting. He'd applied for a transfer to his dream job – a spot in the President's protection detail – and was anticipating the news of the transfer. Was. Until a moment of anger cost him everything he'd worked his entire career for. Nearly a decade of climbing the ranks of the Secret Service, blown in a momentary lapse in self control. He silently rehearsed his apology. Perhaps he could save his career even if it was too late to save the transfer. There'd be other opportunities.

I apologize, sir, for my astounding lapse of judgment.

You know my record, sir. It will never happen again.

The monster deserved it.

He rubbed his hands over his face. He'd been on administrative leave ever since he'd punched a handcuffed mass murderer in the nose. But the guy had been bragging about how he'd murdered Rick's partner, and taunting him with the gory details. Rick really couldn't muster enough regret to make it believable.

I wonder if the Franklin PD takes washed up Secret Service agents. Going back home to Indiana might not be his first choice, but he couldn't envision any life outside law enforcement.

"Agent McCoy, the director will see you now."

"Thank you, Lacey." Rick nodded to the secretary absently and stood, squaring his shoulders and taking a deep breath. *Dear Lord, don't let me get fired here.*

He entered the director's office and closed the door behind him. His boss sat behind his desk, which was covered in neat stacks of papers and folders, as usual. What wasn't usual was the man that also sat on his boss's desk, perched on the corner.

"Agent Patrick McCoy, I'd like you to meet Agent Dante Brand, top agent of our PNI Division." The director gestured to the young man sitting on the corner of his desk. Brand couldn't be more than twenty, with an easy smile, flaming red hair that was fashionably spiked, and strange golden eyes that glittered as if they harbored a secret joke. He wore an incredibly expensive suit unlike anything Rick had seen before. A deep blue tailored cashmere suit jacket, detailed with hand embroidery on the sleeve cuffs and lapels, covering a burgundy silk shirt. The kid literally wore white kid gloves embroidered with an orange and yellow design Rick couldn't make out.

Top agent, my eye. Probably the son of some senator or something handed a made up rank to make daddy happy. Rick crossed the room, forced a smile, and extended his hand to the other agent. "Please, call me Rick."

"I'm Dante, if you please." The other agent took his hand. The gloves were soft, but the kid's handshake was firm, and his voice quietly confident. He had a faint accent – French, maybe – but only as much as you'd expect from someone who had been in the country a while. So a diplomat's kid maybe? Rick cringed inwardly. He was going to be assigned to babysit some pampered rich brat as penance for punching the guy who got his kicks murdering his last partner. A horrible thought struck him. What if he lost this one, too? Would he create an international incident if he couldn't keep the kid out of trouble?

"Dante's going to be your new partner. Don't let his appearance fool you, he outranks you, and will be taking the lead on most of your cases." The director motioned for them to sit. Dante returned to his perch on the corner of the desk, while Rick lowered himself slowly into a plush armchair.

"Director Leon, sir, can we discuss this?" Rick swallowed. He prayed fervently that the PNI Division only took cases like treed cats and missing lunch money. He couldn't risk losing another partner, especially not some juvenile political asset.

"Absolutely, Dante and I both want to be sure you understand fully what you're in for." The director seemed sober as he nodded to Dante. "To begin with, Dante is considerably older than he looks, and has been with the Service far longer than you have. He's quite skilled at what he does, so you don't need to worry about this being a babysitting assignment, or whatever you were thinking."

"I didn't say that." Rick narrowed his eyes. Perhaps he had thought it too loudly. There was no way the baby-faced agent watching him with laughing golden eyes was more experienced than he was. "What is the PNI Division?"

"Paranormal Investigations. We're like Ghostbusters." Dante grinned, his lilting accent making it hard for Rick to decide if he was being serious or not.

"Okay." Rick drew the word out skeptically. "Is that what happened then, you discovered the Fountain of Youth, or the Painting of Dorian Gray, or something?"

"I was cursed, yes. I already was immortal. I made the mistake of thinking myself more beautiful than a fae and was cursed to spend my immortality as a human." Dante frowned and picked an invisible speck of dust off his outrageously expensive suit.

You have to be kidding me. Rick took a deep breath and closed his eyes for a moment to collect his temper. He didn't particularly like being messed with. "Director, I'd like to submit my resignation. Effective immediately. I'll be moving back home to be closer to my parents."

"Don't be that way, Rick." The director pushed a pile of papers toward him. "The position will be a promotion for you, as well as a drastic increase in pay. It'll take some adjusting to, but Dante believes you're the best man for the job, and he's rarely wrong."

"I'm frankly not sure that's a compliment, sir." Rick pushed the words through clenched teeth. "I'll admit I'm less than sorry I punched that murderer, but I don't think I deserve being made the bodyguard for a mentally ill diplomat's kid playing cops and robbers."

Dante laughed aloud, his laugh as musical as his voice. "That is a new one. My last partner thought I was a 'reject from a boy band.'"

"Then what are you? Really? No experienced agent wears clothes like that. No one I know wears clothes like that." Rick gestured to the brightly embroidered suit. "Goodwill or Spirit Halloween?" He knew full well that get up cost more than he made in a month, but he was getting angry with the whole thing.

Dante bristled. "I'll have you know this suit was handcrafted on Saville Row to my custom specifications." His accent thickened and he pulled his right glove off as he spoke. "I suppose they all need proof."

"What are you going to do? Challenge me to a duel at thirty paces?"

"Rick, please," The director admonished.

"No, Charles, this is my responsibility." Dante waved the director off with his loose glove, then fixed his sharp eyes on Rick. "If I were to challenge you to a duel, the Service would lose a good man, and I would still be looking for a partner." He picked up a polished wood paperweight off the desk with his bare hand. The paperweight burst into flames in his hand. He watched it burn until it was a pile of ashes in his hand, dumped the ashes into the trash can, then carefully replaced his glove.

"So you're a magician?" Rick made another dig, even as fear nagged at the back of his mind. What was he dealing with?

"*Mince.*" Dante looked at him with some consternation, the smile on his young face fading slightly.

The director, on the other hand, just laughed. "I'm sorry, Dante, but this is always my favorite part."

"You know how much I hate it, Charles," Dante rebuked him with a sniff of wounded pride. "It would be far easier if I did not have to find a new partner so soon after resurrecting. They never take me seriously."

"What happened, if you don't mind telling me?" Rick ignored the part about 'resurrecting.' The kid had already claimed to be an immortal, and he didn't even begin to know how to deal with that. Lost partners, *that* he was intimately familiar with.

"My partner was taken by a vampire. I was forced to incinerate his body myself to spare him an eternity as one of those foul creatures. The coven descended on me, and while they don't fancy the taste of my blood, they have no qualms about spilling it. I burned one of them before I died, and the rest when I resurrected." Dante gave him a look that challenged him to contradict him, to invalidate his grief. Rick wasn't interested. His own grief was still fresh enough he recognized it when he saw it in another man's eyes.

"I don't believe any of this. I'm a Baptist," Rick replied weakly. He had so many questions and didn't even know how to begin. He picked the most pressing. "Why me?"

"Dante prefers his partners either experienced in law enforcement or in paranormal activity." The director tapped a folder with Rick's name on it with his index finger.

"The LEOs tend to live longer," Dante interrupted.

"He also prefers them to be grounded in religion."

"They tend to adapt faster and be less attracted to the darkness." Dante made a disgusted face that indicated a bad past experience.

Rick wasn't sure he wanted to know what was worse than vampires sucking the blood from your partner.

"I also like my partners to be loyal and not afraid of taking harsh action if necessary. We're not dealing with normal human criminals here." Dante grinned widely at him. "I need a partner willing to punch a lich in the nose for killing me."

Rick blushed. So his little indiscretion had been a deciding factor in his transfer, just not in the way he'd thought. "But what good is a human partner to you? Don't you want another immortal flame thrower?"

"I am a one thousand year old phoenix cursed to a human form. There are no others like me." Dante's voice grew soft and his expression grim.

"Oh. I'm sorry." Rick wasn't sure what he expected Dante to be, but it wasn't *that*. "That explains the fire, then, and the immortality. But you *can* die?"

"I can, and do quite frequently." Dante made a sour face. "It's unpleasant and costly. I try to avoid it when I can. I once managed to survive for thirty years. My shortest survival was about three minutes."

"I remember that. The wizard was waiting when you resurrected." The director turned to Rick. "That's where your job will be different than you're used to. You'll provide investigative and tactical support for Dante on a wide range of cases, obviously, but he'll make the suicide play if necessary. If he dies, you'll have less than thirty seconds to clear a perimeter, or remove his body from the danger zone in any way necessary. The flames from his resurrection incinerate everything within a ten foot radius. Remember the 9/11 conspiracies? Yeah. He and another agent were killed trying to get people out of that mess."

"You'll also want to make sure you're out of the resurrection zone yourself," Dante added softly.

"And that there are no lingering threats to his safety." The director made a wry face. "Or to aid in retrieving his body. One werewolf mafioso got the bright idea to tie him to a concrete block and drop him in the middle of Lake Michigan. He couldn't resurrect until we located him and brought him to the surface."

"Thank God my partner noted the place I went down." Dante gave the director a grateful smile.

"He'll be alert after the flames die down, but generally irritable and may not remember the things that happened immediately before his death."

"Charles, I am only 'generally irritable' because I don't like dying, and awakening to find my clothes destroyed is both mortifying and expensive." Dante laughed and gestured to Rick. "Tell me, Patrick, would you not also be irritable to be shot, awakened naked in the street, and short a ten thousand dollar suit?"

"Rick, and yeah, that would be irritating – if I owned a suit worth even remotely *close* to ten thousand dollars." Rick took a deep breath and counted to ten to take the edge of sarcasm out of his voice. He didn't entirely succeed. "So, the same job I've been doing for nine years, but with monsters and a partner who spontaneously combusts when killed."

"Essentially." The director slapped a sticky note with a single phone number written on it onto the top file in the stack he'd given him. "My personal cell phone number. I want you to at least read the file and consider it. I was Dante's partner until I took this position, so I know it's a lot to take in. If you have any questions, feel free to call me anytime." He stood and extended his hand. "I really do hope you take the job, Rick, but I know it's a lot. I'll give you until the beginning of the week to make up your mind."

"Thanks, Director." Rick shook his director's hand and scooped up the pile of papers. Baptist or not, he was curious enough to at least read the file. "I'm guessing I can't tell anyone else about this?"

"New job, new partner, not sure you're the right fit – you can say whatever you like as long as you leave out the weird stuff." The director waved a hand. "Not that they'll believe you. As soon as you walk out of here, you'll doubt you believe you."

"Wonderful." Rick extended a hand to Dante, then retracted it quickly when he remembered what his touch did to the paperweight.

"I assure you I am no threat to you." Dante laughed, took Rick's hand in both of his, and shook it vigorously. "I look forward to working with you."

"I'll... Pray about it." Rick looked down at the papers in his hands and shook his head. He had a lot of reading and praying to do tonight.

Chapter Two

"He handled that well." Dante meant that quite sincerely as he sat in one of the armchairs facing Charles's desk and swung one leg over the arm. It wasn't entirely unheard of for candidates to refuse or even flee once they knew what he was. It had taken three interviews for him to settle on his last partner. Or rather for his last partner to settle on him.

Agent McCoy was spotless on paper, apart from his recent indiscretion, which Dante found rather endearing. The agent had broad shoulders, thick arms, and wide fists in contrast to Dante's slender and lithe figure. He wore an intentional scruff of a brown beard, khakis, a solid colored dress shirt with the top button unbuttoned and the sleeve cuffs unbuttoned and rolled up past his elbows. Sharp brown eyes, a firmly set jaw, and an impeccable reputation as an investigator hinted at an intensity of character disguised by his casual dress. He gave every impression of a man able to take care of himself in this difficult field. Exactly what Dante was looking for.

"I'm not sure about this, *Chaud*." Charles used his familiar nickname for Dante to signal the conversation was shifting from official to friendly. "He's a skeptic. Agent Azusa was a skeptic, and look what happened. If we'd paid attention to the signs with Azusa–"

"Wes was only a skeptic about *me*, and *he* interviewed better than you did if I recall." Dante chuckled at the memory of Charles' first interview. He'd adamantly refused to believe any of it and barely took the file offered to him, only to return the next day with a five page report on how they weren't utilizing Dante's skills effectively. "Wes was not you, and Agent McCoy is not Wes."

"He'll be gone in a week."

"He's not Madison either.

"He won't be able to handle the resurrections."

"*No one* is able to handle my resurrections. Not at first. You know that as well as anyone."

"What if–"

"He's not Gilles either, *Glace*." Dante sat up with a sigh. *Chaud* and *Glace* – fire and ice – had been their nicknames for each other when he and Charles had been partners. He'd been the passionate, flamboyant one and Charles the cold, calculating one. Playing the opposite was not quite comfortable for him. "It's been eight months. I need a partner to do my job. Keeping me at the desk is not an effective use of my skills, and sending me out alone is too dangerous." This was nothing Charles didn't know himself.

"I don't want to get this wrong." Charles ran his hands over his weary face.

"I'm rarely wrong." Dante gave a cocky half smile as he stood to go. "After meeting Agent McCoy, I am quite confident I am not wrong now."

RICK GOT THROUGH THE papers at two a.m. He dropped his head back on the headboard of his bed and stared at the ceiling. If the paperwork was to be believed, the baby-faced Dante Brand had an impressive service record going all the way back to President Washington. Before that, he'd been in the employ of the French government going back to Leonardo DiVinci. He'd fled Revolutionary France when the French government started oppressing the Church. He was a staunch Roman Catholic and faithful member of one of the oldest churches in Washington DC. He made a mental note to call the church in the morning to make an appointment with the priest to check Dante's back story. Rick wasn't sure what was harder to believe, all this stuff about vampires and cursed phoenixes, or that a Baptist was considering going to a Catholic Priest for advice.

In the meantime, the director *had* said to call anytime. He dialed up the number on the sticky note, ignoring the time glowing on the digital clock on his bedside table.

"Rick."

"Uh. Good morning, Director." Rick stammered, a bit less certain about his plan of action now that he heard the sleep in his boss's voice. "How did you know it was me?"

The director chuckled. "It was three in the morning when I got up the courage to call my predecessor. I wasn't going to wait up for you, but I knew it was coming."

"You were his partner?" Rick wasn't sure how to address the weirdness, or what he even hoped for from this conversation, but talking to someone who had been in his position helped.

"For nearly two decades before I took this promotion. If I wasn't pushing sixty, I'd take my old position back in a heartbeat."

"You really expect me to believe he's... immortal?" Rick nearly choked on the word. He pinched himself hard, hoping to wake up, but only managing to leave a bright red welt on the back of his hand.

"You can believe it or not. That doesn't change the truth. But that's not to say it isn't hard watching him die everytime." The director's voice grew softer at the memories. "Paranormals – they like to be called mythics – do some disturbing damage to their victims."

"How often does he die?" Rick pinched his eyes closed at the rush of memories of his last partner dying in his arms. He couldn't do that over and over again, even *if* Dante did resurrect.

"Depends. We had one case where he died four times in one day. He was incredibly irritated by the end of that day. Another time, he went three years. Most of the mythics know what happens when he resurrects and don't want it to happen anymore than he does, but a few will try to kill him for sport or out of spite."

"Vampires, Director? Paranormals? Immortal phoenixes that burst into flames?" Rick's voice rose in spite of himself. "That's fairy tale stuff. How am I supposed to get around that?"

"If it helps, forget I said any of that, and I'll try again." The director cleared his voice. "Agent McCoy, one of my best agents needs a new partner. In spite of his appearance, he's one of the most experienced and skilled agents we have. Because of his special skill set, you'll be assigned cases that are hard for other teams to handle. I'll expect the two of you to have each other's backs in whatever way necessary." The director paused for a moment. "Is that easier to accept?"

Rick grunted. When put that way, it just sounded like a transfer to an elite investigative unit. "What's he like to work with?"

"Basically what you saw tonight. Easygoing, jovial, unless provoked. The most loyal and devoted partner you'll ever have. The Service literally is his life. He is incredibly vain, which I gather is how he ended up human in the first place, and can be rather overprotective. Because he is immortal, he tends to treat humans like glass. It gets irritating when he insists on taking all the risks, especially if he's jeopardizing the case to do it. I'll expect you to call him out on that."

"What did you tell him about me?" Rick asked, curious because the director's assessment was rather bipolar in its description of the other agent.

"He only asked if you were 'a just man.'" The director laughed. "I think after working with humans for more than half a century, he's quite aware the big ask is coming from him. He's not overly worried about your particular quirks unless they're likely to get you killed."

"Tell him I basically live out of my Jeep and my most expensive suit cost me six hundred dollars. My strong point is investigation and I don't like being told how to do my job." Rick yawned. "I'll give it a try, Director. I can't say that I buy into all the mythic stuff, so you'll pardon me if I'm not particularly eager to test his immortality anytime soon, but he sounds like a good man, and I'm always up for a good partner."

"Get some sleep then, Rick. I'll assign you your first case in the morning."

Chapter Three

Morning came way sooner than Rick anticipated. His phone rang at five in the morning from a number he didn't recognize. He ignored it the first time, but reluctantly picked it up the second.

"McCoy." He groggily squinted at the digital clock beside his bed. It was going to be a long day.

"Rick, this is Dante. Charles gave me your number." Agent Brand's soft voice greeted him. "He said you were willing to give it a shot, so we have a case, if you're up to it. A murder victim was found behind Carlo's Pizzeria when he came in to open it this morning."

"Give me half an hour to shower and dress, and I'll be there." Rick hung up, wondered briefly how long it took Dante to primp in the morning, decided that kind of speculation probably wasn't a good way to start their partnership, and threw off the covers to get going.

After his shower, he shot off a text to his girlfriend, Gracie. He'd come to DC expecting discipline, and got a job offer instead. He needed to talk to her, but she probably wasn't even up yet, and likely wouldn't have time to talk before she started teaching her kindergarten class anyway. MEETING WENT WELL. GOT A PROMOTION. CALL ME AFTER SCHOOL. Satisfied that the text sounded appropriately upbeat, Rick pocketed his phone and got in the car.

He stopped at a coffee shop on his way and got a cup of the biggest, strongest coffee they offered for himself and caramel macchiato for Dante. Not that he had any idea what his new partner drank, he just couldn't see someone as prissy as Agent Brand taking his black, and going full snowflake with a soy milk latte seemed a bit too far.

He got to the scene to find it already cordoned off and a team of uniformed police officers running the perimeter. He flashed his badge to the nearest officer and carefully made his way to where Dante was crouched next to a body.

"Catch me up." Rick offered the drink to Dante who thanked him, but didn't even ask what it was.

"Night shift manager. She lived alone and wasn't missed when she didn't come home last night. Carlo came to open for the day and found her like this. He called the police and they called us."

"It looks pretty cut and dried to me." Rick leaned forward to look at the body. It was a short, heavyset woman with her hair pulled back in a tight ponytail. She wore the uniform of the pizzeria and black industrial loafers. It looked like she'd been attacked by a stray dog. There were defensive bite marks on her hands and arms, and while they bled profusely, they weren't the cause of death. The dog had apparently gotten her down and went for her throat. It was a terrible way to go, sure, but nothing really "paranormal" about it. "She probably smelled like food when she left the store. A hungry stray attacked and she tried to defend herself. Why call you instead of animal control?"

"We requested the case." Dante pulled a silver pen from his jacket pocket and used it to point to the wounds. "These bite marks are larger than any normal stray would make, and it is rare for a stray dog to go in for the kill like that. We have staff who monitor police bands for cases like this and notify us so we can request jurisdiction. They rarely complain."

"Okay." Rick drew the word out slowly. "What else do we have?"

Dante sat back on his heels and looked up at him. "Local LEOs canvassed the scene for clues, but found nothing helpful. The owner of the restaurant is inside, if you would have any questions?"

"What questions are we going to ask? Have you seen any gigantic strays hanging around?" Rick lowered his voice. "Are we pretending all our cases are normal, or going with the werewolf attack theory?"

"You may do as you like." Dante gave him a wide smile as he stood to his feet and straightened his suit, the same one he'd worn the previous day, but with a tan turtleneck. "Let me warn you, though, that this case will be solved much quicker if we approach it as a murder."

"How about a friendly bet?" Rick smiled back. "If it's a perfectly non-paranormal explanation, you buy me dinner. If it ends up being an episode of X-files, I'll buy."

"I hope you're flush at the moment, my favorite French diner is rather expensive." Dante opened the door to the diner and gestured to a distraught, red-faced man sitting at one of the tables. "Monsignor Carlo, I am deeply sorry for your loss." Dante bowed to the man slightly and spoke to him in what Rick guessed to be Italian. He handed him his own handkerchief to dry his eyes instead of the coarse cloth table napkin, then switched to English. "My name is Dante Brand, and this is my partner Rick McCoy. We are here to help the police investigate what happened."

Rick tried not to roll his eyes. Most of the international restaurant owners were at least second generation Americans and couldn't speak their native language any better than Rick could.

"Grazi." Carlo's accent was thicker than Dante's and he sounded truly grateful for Dante's thoughtfulness. "She was my wife's sister. How am I going to explain this to her?"

"We are still trying to explain it ourselves." Dante sat across from him at the table, took a notepad from the inside pocket of his jacket, and opened the notepad. "Have you noticed anything strange around the restaurant lately?"

"Nothing like this, no. This is a fine Italian neighborhood." Carlo swore in Italian. "We have our problems, but nothing like this."

"The Vizzini's make sure of it, no?" Dante's soft voice grew softer, more sympathetic.

Now Rick did raise an eyebrow. The Vizzini family was a local crime family. Did Dante think this was a mob shakedown?

"Giancarlo is a personal friend. The family is not involved here." Carlo bristled. "Angela was even seeing Joey Vizzini."

"Everything was good between her and her boyfriend?" Rick asked. Mob bosses were completely within the normal realm and something he was very comfortable with.

"Eh. Better than some of my employees' relationships. Everyone has problems, you know?" Carlo shrugged and frowned. "But I don't think Joey would sic a dog on her."

Rick thought of his text to Gracie and agreed. Every relationship had problems, but Gracie wouldn't sic a dog on him for transferring to DC without discussing it with her... Though she might break up with him. The thought turned his stomach, and he surreptitiously slid his phone from his pocket to glance at the screen. Nothing yet.

"Thank you." Dante snapped the notebook closed and stood abruptly. "We will let you know if we discover anything."

He left the restaurant quickly with Rick at his heels. Something Carlo had said meant something to the flamboyant agent, but for the life of him Rick couldn't figure out what.

"We need to speak with Joey Vizzini immediately. Can you drive?" Dante asked urgently as they left the restaurant.

"Yeah, my car is parked out front. Commando Green Jeep." Rick pulled his keys and hit the unlock button. The car chirped and flashed its headlights. "What happened?"

"I will tell you, but you will not like the explanation." Dante kept his voice low as if not wanting to be overheard. "Every major mythic race is separated into guilds and aligned with a human guild. Werewolves are aligned with the Italian mafia."

"Of course they are." Rick muttered. He yanked open his door and climbed in the driver's seat. *I wonder how expensive French restaurants really are, because I'm absolutely losing this bet.*

"If one of the other families ordered one of their dogs to attack Joey Vizzini's girlfriend, this may already be out of our hands." Dante stopped at one of the squad cars and lifted a leather carry on garment bag from the trunk. "One of your... less common duties will be caretaker of my spare suit. May I put it in your trunk?"

"Sure. No problem. I always carry my partner's luggage." Rick grunted as he clicked the unlock button on his key fob. He'd only been on the job for a couple hours and it was already getting harder to pretend this was a normal assignment. He was going to need another coffee before lunch at this rate. He popped the rear hatch open and gestured for Dante to wedge his garment bag between several bags of groceries. "Eating out is too expensive."

Dante nodded sympathetically and slid his bag inside. "When I die, you will need to clear the area, eliminate the threat, and have my clothes ready. I cannot stress this enough."

"I don't intend for that to be necessary." Rick sighed and rounded to his door. "But the director did mention it."

"The director always mentions it." Dante sighed as he slammed the hatch shut and went to the passenger side. "And yet, the first time they always forget..." Dante trailed off as he looked at the trash cluttering the floor of the passenger's side.

"Sorry about that." Rick brushed a crumpled bag of taco takeout off the seat onto the floor. "It's been a while since I had a passenger."

"I think I will walk." Dante looked at the trash like it was going to jump up and bite him. "I can give you the address and meet you there."

"Don't be a drama queen. It's just a bit of garbage. You're an immortal mythical creature and your weakness is *garbage*?" Rick glared at him. "Besides, is this urgent or not? What happens if this Joey Vizzini decides to send one of his 'werewolves' to avenge his girl before we get there?"

Dante looked up at him with a murderous glare, but gingerly kicked the trash aside and sat in the seat.

"To answer your question, that would depend entirely on whether they know whose werewolf is to blame." Dante frowned. "If they do – or think they do – this will not be the first murder."

"Delightful. Can you get us there?" Rick gave up trying to fight the whole "mythic" thing. Whether Dante was talking about werewolves or trained attack dogs didn't change their job here. Either way, the person behind the attack needed to be found and stopped.

"Giancarlo Vizzini and I have a history." Dante gestured gracefully with a gloved hand. "I've been there many times."

"Delightful," Rick repeated and threw the car in gear. In spite of his skepticism, he found himself wondering how long he could keep his new partner alive, and what exactly would happen when he failed.

DANTE DIRECTED RICK to an asymmetrical mansion surrounded by a large brick wall with an iron gate. Rick flashed his badge at the guard in the gate house, who only hesitated long enough to see Dante in the car beside him.

"Good afternoon, Essex." Dante leaned around his new partner and greeted the young werewolf. "We need to speak to Joey on business. Can you announce us?"

"I'm pretty sure I heard Mr. Vizzini tell you he'd have your throat ripped out if you ever set foot on his land again, Mr. Brand." The young guard looked uncomfortable, as if he were concerned he'd be the one ordered to tear out Dante's throat himself.

As it should be. Dante smiled easily. If he must die repeatedly, at least he was blessed to do so in a way that made his enemies think twice before killing him.

"I'm afraid we bring some difficult news for Joey Vizzini." Dante pulled the fingers of his glove off his left hand. "I suppose I can open the gate the same way I did last time."

"Nn-No, Mr. Brand, that's fine." The guard scrambled back to the gate house and pushed the intercom, spoke a few words, then buzzed them in.

"Out of curiosity," Rick pulled forward as the gates opened, and flicked a glance at Dante's hand as he pulled the glove back on. "How did your little flash paper trick get you through before?"

"I melted through the hinges." Dante schooled his face to hide the mixture of amusement and consternation he felt. Some of his partners were much more resistant to the truth about what he was. Those usually struggled the hardest the first time they watched him die. If Agent McCoy persisted in denying the obvious, he was headed for a very difficult awakening. "I assure you that my powers are not a trick, and this job will be far easier for you when you accept that."

"Advanced technology, then, or some exceptional skill with a lighter. I'm not saying you don't have a useful skill, because that guard was clearly afraid of you." Agent McCoy's knuckles grew white as he gripped the steering wheel. "I'm just not buying that it's magic or alchemy or whatever."

Dante shrugged. Agent McCoy would believe soon enough. *Gracious God, soften the blow.*

They pulled up in front of the house and got out of the car. The door opened before they even made their way up the stone steps to the porch. An older man whose Ralph Lauren polo and carefully manicured appearance covered a body wasted by self indulgence waited for them with a sour expression. A belligerent young man wearing distasteful leather and mesh clubwear stood behind the older man.

"Brand. I told you to never show your face here again." Giancarlo Vizzini glared at Dante and kept one hand on the door frame to block Joey in with his arm. He sized up Agent McCoy and dismissed him with a sniff. He tilted his head toward his son without taking his eyes of Dante. "Joey, get Farkas and Chann. Tell them I have a peacock for them to snack on."

"I'd advise against that, Mr. Vizzini." Agent McCoy deftly pulled his badge with one hand and patted the very visible butt of his holstered handgun with the other. "We're here on official business, and if you sic your dogs on us we will shoot them."

"Have fun with that, officer." Vizzini barked a harsh laugh and turned back to Dante. "New partner, eh? What'd you do to the last one?"

"Agent McCoy is quite capable, I assure you." *At least he will be when he catches up.* Dante pulled off his right glove with a frown and gestured to the mafioso. "And you are fully aware of my capabilities. We won't take much of your time."

"We're actually here to speak with Joey." Rick nodded to the younger man. "Are you still dating Amara Zanotti?"

"Maybe. What's she saying about me?" Joey's belligerent tone matched his posture as he folded his arms over his chest and leaned against the door frame.

"I'm afraid that Ms. Zanotti was attacked and killed by a dog late last night." Rick softened his tone. "We were wondering if you had any idea who might have wanted her dead?"

The Vizzinis changed their posture as soon as Agent McCoy said the word "dog." Their eyes darted to Dante, who simply nodded slowly to acknowledge the subtext Agent McCoy was missing. Both Vizzinis knew that Dante only handled mythic crimes, so would logically know what kind of dog they were discussing in this context.

"Thanks for the news, officers." Giancarlo tried to back his visibly shaken son back into the house and close the door. "We'll handle this in house."

"I'm afraid that's not how things work, Mr. Vizzini." Agent McCoy reacted before Dante did and wedged his foot in the door. "I'd hate to have to bring your son downtown as a person of interest in the case."

"Or be back here arresting one of you for the next murder." Dante gestured his gloveless hand. "I believe PNI has proven its competence more than once. Let us handle this."

Giancarlo Vizzini grunted, but didn't open the door any further. "Giuseppe Ciccarelli was jealous that Amara picked my Joey instead of him. Wharton is the biggest and meanest of all of them, and is especially attached to Giuseppe. He probably *liked* taking out that girl."

Joey made a garbled squeak and vanished into the house.

"You got a week, Brand." Vizzini growled. "If you haven't made an arrest by then, me and my dogs are going to have a conference with Ciccarelli and demand Wharton be put down – or else we'll do it for him." He kicked Agent McCoy's foot out of the way, slammed the door, and clicked the lock in place.

"That seems pretty clear cut to me." Agent McCoy shrugged as they turned back down the stairs toward his car. "Jealous love triangle gone wrong. Nothing weird about that. I like my steak well done, by the way."

Dante hummed softly as he replaced his glove. He'd not bother disillusioning the skeptical agent about Wharton's real identity at the moment. "Perhaps. Though a week still doesn't give us much time. We should probably try to meet with Ciccarelli and Wharton yet today."

Chapter Four

Rick was feeling a bit more confident in his chances of getting a steak dinner instead of French cuisine by the time they left the Vizzinis'. Other than being a bit weird about Dante's admittedly impressive fire trick, the Vizzinis never suggested anything was out of the normal realm. They never questioned the attack dog theory or suggested it was a werewolf like Dante did. In fact, they seemed to know immediately who was behind the dog attack. Who knows. Maybe Dante was one of those quirky agents that is so good at what he does, people just look past his oddities – like Columbo, Monk, or Poirot. Maybe he was self conscious about the disrespect his baby face earned him, so came up with the immortal story to get people off his back.

That had to be it.

They left the Vizzinis' mansion compound and went somewhere about as far opposite as you could get: a rundown boxing gym in a clearly less reputable part of town.

"The city's second largest crime boss runs a gym?" Rick looked the place over skeptically as they parked. He decided to lock the car and set the alarm with a click and beep of his key fob.

"Underground fight club, actually." Dante brushed an invisible speck of dust off his pants as they approached the door. "If people will bet on it, they fight it here – dogs, cocks, MMA, werewolves–"

"Phoenix?" Rick teased. He couldn't possibly see the prissy, vain agent involved in a fight club.

Dante just gave him a bright grin with a bit of mischief in his eye. "You know what they say about fight club, no?"

"Get out. You? Fighting for fun?" Rick tried to imagine the pretty federal agent with a black eye and fat lip, and failed. "You're kidding me."

"You underestimate me because of my appearance." Dante sobered and his voice took a hard edge. "Perhaps a couple rounds together after we are done today would help your skepticism."

"Gloves on and spotted, sure. If you don't think it'll hurt your pride too much when I wipe the mat with you." Rick wasn't exactly sure flooring his new partner the first day was a great way to build rapport, but it seemed to be the first point of common interest they'd found. "I had a bit of a reputation in the ring in New York."

"I am well aware of your reputation. In spite of that, I will try to go easy on you." Dante pushed the gym door open to signal the conversion had ended.

Rick fell back a step and stared at his partner's back. Was that hubris or banter? It hadn't really sounded like either. Dante sounded like he seriously believed he would have to pull his punches in a ring with the best cruiserweight boxer in the New York branch. Maybe Vizzini was right to call Dante a peacock. It could be fun to take him down a peg, though Rick doubted the other agent's pride would survive the fight.

They entered the gym with barely a second look from the heavyweight watching the door, and went straight to the business office without confrontation. Dante knocked on the door and a voice on the other side gruffly welcomed them in.

"Dante!" A slight man with a forearm crutch rounded the desk enthusiastically as they entered. "Please, tell me you're here about the fight. I've already started taking bets, but my patrons are always eager to put fresh money on the big fights."

"I'm afraid our visit is more business than pleasure, Chick. This is my partner, Agent McCoy. Agent McCoy, this is Giovanni Ciccarelli."

Dante paused while the pair shook hands, then addressed Ciccarelli again, "Is Giuceppe or Wharton around?"

Ciccarelli's face fell. "My son's a good boy, Dante, and Wharton keeps him out of trouble. What do you need them for?"

"Has your son ever mentioned an Amara Zanotti?" Rick didn't miss the difference between how Ciccarelli and Vizzini reacted to Dante, and he did wonder at it a little. If they were supposed to be rival crime families, why was his new partner on such good terms with the Ciccarellis?

"He mighta." Ciccarelli frowned at Dante. "Do we need a lawyer? 'Business' means I need a lawyer."

"That would depend entirely on whether Giuceppe and Wharton can account for their whereabouts last night between midnight and three." Dante shrugged carelessly, but Rick noticed him fingering the embroidered hem of his glove. Perhaps he was not on as friendly terms as he pretended.

"You'll have to ask them." Ciccarelli shrugged and went back to his seat. "Your new partner knows the risks of being your partner?"

"There are always risks in our job." Dante's voice grew cold and he didn't look at Rick. "He's an experienced LEO, he understands that."

"How long did Madison last? Regan? That tiny girl you were with at our last fight? I can't even remember their names, there have been so many."

"Charles Leon was my partner for nineteen years, and is doing quite well." Dante's voice was as soft and polite as always, but his face was pale and his fists trembled at his sides.

"I've read Agent Brand's file," Rick interrupted, hoping to draw the attention away from his partner. Whatever the source of Dante's flame-throwing abilities, letting this masterpiece of human manipulation goad him into using them wouldn't end well for any of them. "I know his history and he knows mine, which has a few spots of its own."

"Then you read about Iscariot, didn't you?" Ciccarelli smiled at Rick in a decidedly unfriendly way. When Rick simply scrambled to recall the name, Ciccarelli's smile widened. "You'll have to ask Brand to introduce you at some point so you can compare notes."

Rick didn't remember reading about a partner named "Iscariot", and given the religious subtext of the name wondered if it was a reference to the circumstances rather than the guy's actual name.

It meant something to Dante, though, because the blood flooded back to match his face to his hair. His partner muttered, "St. Jerome, give me grace," then placed his hands – still gloved, thankfully – on the edge of the desk and leaned forward. He said something in harsh, clipped Italian, in a tone far different than he had used with the pizzeria owner.

He got a far different response as well. Ciccarelli grunted a single word in Italian, one Rick was certain he didn't want to add to his vocabulary, and gestured to the door. "Giuceppe is in the basement getting ready for tonight's bout. Wharton is probably with him. I'll send them both to meet you in the parking lot. I'll not have you messing up my carpet."

Dante stood, straightened his suit, and nodded. "PNI appreciates your cooperation, Chick."

"Anytime, Brand." Ciccarelli's smile returned more tightly. "And my gym looks forward to the next time you want to fight."

"You have nice friends." Rick jerked his head toward the building as they walked back out to the parking lot.

"Ah, when Charles said that my enemies are usually as reluctant to kill me as I am to die, he did not include Vizzini and Ciccarelli." Dante curled his lip in disgust. "Once my human enemies have cause to realize what I am, they often come to take pleasure in taking me out. Life is cheap, especially when death is transient."

"You mean I might have to watch your back because one of these guys might try to off you for kicks?" Rick cast a wary glance back at the

36

building as a pair of men exited. One was young, about the age of Joey Vizzini, with black hair, olive skin tone, and the same sullen expression. The other was a gruff man in his mid-thirties, with unruly brown hair, a stubbly beard, and a look of pure hatred on his face.

"Especially these guys," Dante murmured as he turned to address the newcomers. "Giuseppe, Wharton."

"Chick says you think I killed some cheap slut." The older man – presumably Wharton – got in Dante's face and flashed a set of unnaturally sharp teeth.

"I did not. I asked if Giuceppe knew an Amara Zanotti, and where you two might have been between midnight and three." Dante smiled tightly. "Is there a reason Chick might have jumped to murder?"

Wharton took a step back and glared.

"Sure, Amara and I had a disagreement," Giuceppe interjected, "but I wouldn't kill her."

"We still need to know where you two were last night." Rick edged closer to his partner, a little uneasy about the way the young mobster's bodyguard was eyeing Dante's neck. "And someone else to corroborate."

"I was sleeping, alone." Giuceppe didn't look particularly happy to be admitting that. "Wharton has a room beside mine. Dad's security tapes should show you we didn't leave last night."

"But you'll need a warrant for those." Wharton snarled. "You can get them through the family lawyer. PNI has the contact information."

"Of course." Dante nodded. "You may as well prepare them, since it is in your best interest to produce them. It would make life easier on everyone if you just turned them in."

"Why would I want to make your life easier, Brand?" Wharton gave him a malicious grin as he corralled Giuceppe back toward the building. "Talk to the lawyer. Whoever offed the girl, it wasn't us. You're barking up the wrong tree."

"We shall see," Dante murmured skeptically as he and Rick turned to head toward the car themselves.

"And Brand?" Giuceppe called back over his shoulder. His voice trembled was he spoke. "I'd'a never killed Amara. She was coming back to me after she got tired of Joey. I'm a patient man. I didn't need to kill her."

"And I don't need to waste my time with some cheap slut," Wharton bared his teeth at Dante, "Or a painted peacock. You know our lawyer, Brand. We're done."

The door slammed behind them.

"That went well." Dante shrugged and turned toward the car.

"Because we're not dead yet?" Rick barked a laugh. "I think Wharton wanted a piece of you."

"Wharton and I have an extensive history. If any mythic could be called my enemy, it would certainly be him." Dante frowned. "He sees me as a dog of the human police, just as he is for Chick and his gang. There are many mythics that resent my role, but few who resent it as much as he does."

"Yay," Rick said dryly as he climbed in the driver's seat. "What's next? Call in the warrant and get lunch while we wait?"

"I'll call it in." Dante pulled his phone from his pocket as he got in the passenger seat. "There's a great Hawaiian food truck in town you should try. The Spam Katsu Musubi is especially good."

"Hawaiian sounds good. But spam? I'll pass, thanks. How is that even Hawaiian?" Rick shook his head. "Just tell me where to go."

They located the truck in the parking lot of a government building, and sat at the edge of the fountain in front of the building to eat. While Rick didn't get the Spam Katsu Musubi, he did agree that it was some of the best food he'd ever eaten.

"I'm going to let the fact that at no point have we seen any killer attack dogs slide for just a moment." Rick sucked sticky sauce off his fingers. "You don't actually think that Ciccarelli and his enforcer had anything to do with that murder, do you?"

"Giuceppe seemed sincere enough." Dante frowned at the remains of his meal. "My feelings about Wharton aside, I can't see him acting outside his master's instructions."

"Could Giovanni have ordered a hit to get the girl out of his son's life?" Rick balled up the rest of his trash and shot it into the trash can.

"Possibly." Dante stood and crossed to the can. "Let's try to talk to some others who knew them. Perhaps someone can tell us whether Chick opposed their relationship, or if there was a reason she chose Joey over –"

A crack sounded and Dante jerked backward and fell to the ground beside the fountain, shot clean through the head.

Chapter Five

P anic and a wave of memories rooted Rick to his place, completely forgetting the director's instructions for what to do if Dante died. He lost ten critical seconds staring at Dante's very dead body, trying to neither vomit nor break down into a blubbering pile of tears. Then his training kicked in and he scrambled to reclaim the time limit the director had given him. He wasn't even remotely convinced Dante would resurrect, and the horror of losing his new partner so soon tormented him at the back of his mind, but he knew he had to keep it together to secure the area, like any gunfire situation.

He assessed the area quickly. The director said Dante needed ten feet clearance, but dragging him to an open space would expose Rick to the gunman that took out Dante, a gunman Rick couldn't actually see right now. His only option was to leave Dante and seek a different shelter from both the gunman and Dante's resurrection fire.

Firing in the general area of the shooter, Rick darted to the trash can, sat with his back against the metal cage surrounding it, and dialed the director.

"Director Leon, Dante is down." He risked a glance over at where Dante's body still lay. "A sniper got him."

"How long has it been?" Director Leon didn't even sound fazed.

"Twenty seconds?" Was it thirty? What if he didn't get up? Rick found himself hoping the paranormal was true for the first time in his life.

"You've cleared the resurrection radius?" The director stressed, "*You're* clear of the resurrection radius?"

"Yes." It had to be thirty by now. This was horrible. He was a worthless partner. He was absolutely turning in his resignation the moment he got back. Forget law enforcement. He'd go make pizzas before he did this again.

"Has the threat been neutralized?"

"It's a *sniper*, Director. I can't even see him!" Rick shouted. What was that smell? He glanced back over at Dante to see a spiral of smoke rising from his partner's body.

The director kept talking – something about watching for the sniper to pop up when Dante resurrected – but Rick didn't hear. The smoke had turned into a full blaze, then a blast of fire engulfed the body and lapped at the water surrounding the fountain where they'd been sitting. Rick raised an arm to shield his face from the heat, still uncomfortably hot even from this distance.

The fire died back to a cloud of steam and a ring of blackened cement with Dante standing in the center. He looked around in confusion, then at his missing clothes in dismay.

And a second shot took him out like before.

With a cry, Rick turned and fired in the direction of the shot, getting a satisfying shout in return. It felt like everything he thought he knew had been flipped and it was all he could do not to scream and run. Dante had been standing there, only moments before. He shouldn't have been. He was dead before. There was no question. He was dead *again*. Rick counted down from thirty, even as his hands shook. This was too much. Keeping his mind on the mission was nearly all he could handle. *Take out the sniper and protect Dante. You can regroup later.*

The countdown ended, and the blast of heat hit him again. This time he didn't flinch, keeping his eyes out for the sniper. There! The flash of Dante's resurrection fire glinted off a rifle barrel poking from the third story of the building across the street. Rick fired twice and the rifle fell to the street with a clatter. He holstered his gun, wiped his sweaty palms on his pants, and turned to face his partner.

The confusion on Dante's face faded quickly to irritation. "What just happened?"

"You got sniped. Twice. Don't worry I got him." Rick ran his hand through his hair. "You died. *Graphically.* How am I supposed to get those pictures out of my head? How are you even standing there?"

"Yes, yes. I do this, rather frequently unfortunately." Dante glared. "I need someone to back me up so I *don't* get sniped and graphically murdered twice in one day. That is why you're here, no?"

"I... I just can't. You're lucky I'm even still around now and not halfway back to New York." Rick turned to go. "I'm going back to the hotel. I just need a bit of space." *And a shrink.*

"I see." Dante's tone softened. "Is there any way you can bring me my clothes before you go?"

Rick shook his head. How could a flame throwing immortal be so incredibly helpless? He walked back to where they'd parked, pulled Dante's case from the trunk, and carried it back to where his partner stood in humiliation. He sighed. Like it or not, this guy needed a partner. Rick just wasn't sure he was the right man for the job. "Get dressed. I'll at least take you back to the office before I make up my mind."

❖ ❖ ❖ ❖ ❖

Rick hit the punching bag again. After he'd dropped Dante off at the office, he'd given his resignation to the director and immediately went to the gym. Gracie had texted, then called twice, but he ignored her. The director had offered him a shrink attached to PNI. He probably should have taken him up on it, but the last thing he wanted to do right now was talk about what happened. Right now, all he wanted to do was punch things.

He hit the bag until his hands hurt and sweat soaked his tee shirt. His partner had died. *Twice.* And they expected him to accept this as *normal.* Tyee had bled out in his arms. When Dante had gone down, Rick had nearly come undone. He couldn't take an assignment where watching his partner die was *literally* part of the job description. He'd lose it.

43

He was losing it *now*. He barely noticed when his knuckles started to bleed, and ended up staring too long at the rusty smears on the white bag. He stopped to bandage his hands and kept going. Vampires. Werewolves. Flaming phoenixes in the form of men that resurrect when killed. None of that was real. It *couldn't* be real. Admitting mythical creatures were real went against what he believed about reality.

If he was honest, that was really what was under his skin at the moment. He could adapt to an immortal partner. Knowing Dante would get back up no matter what kind of hit he took would be a relief – once he could get past the gore. Meshing the paranormal with his faith... that would be a bigger hurdle to leap. Making pizzas in Indiana wouldn't create an existential crisis.

Shaking out his hands, he decided to quit before he actually hurt himself. He toweled the sweat from his face and threw the towel across his shoulders. He wasn't in the mood for shower thoughts, though the rank smell from his sweat-saturated shirt warned him he couldn't put it off for long. He'd go back to the hotel, pay-per-view tonight's big UFC fight, order Doordash, and shower when he was too exhausted to think deeply about anything. The fact that the only spiritual counsel he could get on the topic was a Catholic priest didn't help his mood at all. Imagining placing the call back to his home pastor to ask, "what do I do if I see a man rise from the dead," nearly sent him back to the punching bag to finish turning his hands to pulp.

It was dusk when he left the gym, and the outline of a man leaning against the hood of his Jeep was highlighted by the setting sun.

"Yeah, nope," Rick muttered as he recognized the flaming red hair and tailored suit. Fist pulp it was. He briefly wondered if they'd be playing the fight in the ER as he turned back toward the gym.

"Rick please." Dante's soft, lyrical voice followed him. "I'll just take a moment of your time."

Rick stopped, his back to Dante. The last thing he wanted right now was to talk to him. What he wanted was to go back to his hotel and pretend he'd never even met the other man.

"Charles told me you resigned. It is not easy to be my partner, and I understand." Dante's voice lowered to nearly a whisper. "I would just prefer the agency not lose a good agent. I asked Charles to give you the transfer you wanted, if I could persuade you to stay."

Did he even want to stay? A week ago, a transfer sounded like a dream come true. Now Dante's death and resurrection would be haunting his nightmares.

Dante sighed, took one of Rick's hands, and stuffed something into his fist. "Thank you for your trouble. May God bless you wherever your path leads."

Rick looked down at the envelope Dante had left in his hand as the other agent's quiet footfalls retreated. He lifted the flap to see two tickets to the fight.

"Dante, wait." Rick blew a long slow breath through his lips and turned to face the immortal. "How did you get these? They've been sold out for months."

"One cannot live in the city as long as I have without making some friends in high places. After our conversation at Chick's, I thought you'd enjoy the match." Dante flashed him a wide grin. "I hope you don't mind sharing a box with Senator Perez."

Rick gasped and looked at the tickets again. He'd totally missed the box on the printout.

"You might want to shower before you go. I'm fairly certain they'd prefer you didn't smell like the fighters you were going to watch."

"Th-thank you." Rick felt like his life was reeling again.

"All I ask is that you reconsider your resignation, if not as my partner, then at least from the agency at large."

"You'd want me back as your partner? I got you killed. Twice." Rick scoffed. "And nearly left you standing naked in the middle of the street."

"Yes, the latter would have been unforgivable." Dante chuckled softly. "You should ask Charles about his first time. If he will even tell you."

"You're serious. Are all your partner's first times like this?"

"No. Few had the skill to take out a sniper at the distance you did." Dante sobered. "I rarely make the wrong choice for my partner and I don't believe I did now. I would be honored if you accepted the job, but would be satisfied if you at least stayed with the agency."

"I'll think about it." Rick looked down at the tickets. If he hurried, he could shower and change before taking an Uber to the stadium. He certainly wouldn't have time to think about anything at all until after the fight. "You know, Dante. There are two tickets, and you're about the only other person I know here in DC. You wouldn't want to come along, would you?"

"I would enjoy it." Dante rounded Rick's car to the passenger side. "There are rumors the challenger is half yeti, and I'm curious to see if that's true."

"Dante?"

"Hmm?"

"Not helping."

"Right."

Chapter Six

One day was pretty quick to scare off a partner, even for Dante. The first time they watched him die was always shocking. It was simply unfortunate that it had also been the first time Rick's persistence in denying the existence of mythic beings had been challenged as well. At least the fight had persuaded Agent McCoy to hold off on his resignation, and coaxed him into agreeing to the challenge they'd teased at Chick's. They'd agreed to meet before work at the agency gym – a small, but well equipped space in the basement where agents could stay in shape, train, or just blow off steam – and face off for bragging rights.

Rick was already there when Dante arrived. He was wearing a pair of long shorts and a worn tee shirt for a church softball team. Several other agents were buzzing around him as he stretched.

"You're fighting *Dante*?" Ashley from accounting gasped as Dante entered the room and crossed to the mat. The other agents hushed and gathered around the mat.

"Three rounds, two minutes each. Gloves on." Rick nodded to Dante's white gloved hands. "Both sets. No fire tricks." He frowned for a moment as if thinking. "Is there anything else I should know ahead of time? You're not going to burst into flames if I knock you out, are you?"

"Unless you are accustomed to killing your opponents when you fight, no." Dante smiled as he strapped on his head gear. He himself wore bright blue jogging pants with a coordinating tee and matching jacket. Even after several centuries as a human, he still couldn't get past the sheer *nakedness* of human skin and preferred to cover as much of it as he could. "I am faster and stronger than you, but will pull my punches until you show me you can handle it."

"Wow. You certainly don't have a self-esteem problem do you?" Rick laughed as Ashley helped him with his gloves. "Bring your best game, Dante, and I promise not to mess up your pretty face too much."

Dante shrugged and took a defensive stance in the middle of the mat. Rick's file had shown him to be a worthy opponent, but there were significant physical differences between humans and mythics of any race. Still, pride was his ruling passion, and the reason he was human in the first place. He made the sign of the cross and determined not to let his pride lead him into overconfidence.

The fight began with Rick throwing an aggressive jab-cross that Dante blocked easily, but was forceful enough to drive him back a step, and nearly made him miss the left hook Rick followed with. He only partially blocked it, and Rick scored a glancing blow off his headgear.

Rick's mouthguard made further taunting impossible, but he still smiled widely around the guard and saluted Dante with a gloved hand as he ducked out of the way of Dante's return attack.

As Dante had promised, he was faster, and Rick was unable to get his guard back up after his taunt before Dante feinted with his left hand and drove a controlled right hook into his partner's side. Still, it was strong enough to force a surprised grunt from Rick. Rick's eyes narrowed and his smile flattened as he counterpunched with a left jab strong enough to snap Dante's head back.

Warm blood trickled from Dante's nose. He wiped at it ineffectively with his glove and back pedaled. If he'd have been a human, he'd be stretched out on the mat now. How many one punch KOs did Rick have? He was suddenly less concerned about pulling his punches than he had been, short of breaking bone.

Rick won the first match and Dante won the second, due to a lucky left cross that got past Rick's defenses and knocked him on his butt.

During the rest period before the final match, Rick spit out his mouth guard and taunted, "Is that the best you have? A lucky shot? At least you've got your fire and looks going for you. Well, fire at least." He grinned and nodded to Dante's face. "Sorry about the nose. Hopefully by the time we're done, I can give you an eye to match."

Dante spit out his own mouthguard, "My face will heal, but nothing can make up for a mind that functions at six guinea-pig power."

The watching agents laughed and jeered good-naturedly. Even Rick chuckled at his barb. They stood to face off for the final match. Rick's left handedness gave him an unconventional advantage, coupled with the inescapable fact that he might actually be a better fighter than Dante was. That left Dante only with his power and speed to rely on if he wanted to win this final match and the bout. He stepped in quickly and rained a rapid series of jabs and crosses on his partner's face and body – short, fast punches packed with all the power he could pack in without sacrificing speed. The effect was brutal, driving Rick to the edge of the mat and rewarding every attempt he made at an offensive strike with a blow to the head. Rick managed to get Dante's hands in a clinch as he tried to recover from Dante's offensive. His weight was heavier against Dante's arms than it should have been. His partner was flagging. A small smile tugged at the corner of Dante's mouth. Time for the KO. Dante broke his hands free and blocked the desperate, wild right jab Rick threw in response.

Rick's tired face lit with a smile and Dante had half a second to realize his mistake before his partner stepped in and drove a left uppercut into his liver. Excruciating pain radiated through Dante's body and his legs gave out beneath him. He clutched his arm to his side as he curled up against the pain. Something hit the mat beside him, and he was vaguely aware that the countdown started, but he simply couldn't get his body to cooperate enough to get himself back on his feet.

The countdown ended and one of the other agents crossed the mat and offered him a hand up. He waved him off and rolled over onto his back, his left arm still pressed to his side. He spit out his mouth guard and mumbled for them to give him a minute. He was never going to hear the end of losing like this.

"Dang, Dante, you hit hard." Rick groaned beside him.

"*I* hit hard?" Dante turned his head to glare at his partner. "I'm trying to figure out why anyone in their right mind would agree to fight you after watching a single match."

"Gluttons for punishment, I guess." Rick chuckled, then moaned. "I'd like to stay here for a week, thanks. My head feels like someone used it as a bowling ball."

"Wait." Dante rolled over and pushed himself to one elbow gingerly as he finally realized that his partner was *lying* on the mat beside him.

"Double knockout." Rick weakly lifted a still gloved hand. "That uppercut was the last one I had. I could barely see straight to throw it." He offered Dante his fist. "Nice fight, my friend. You're a great fighter behind those fancy clothes and pretty face."

Dante bumped his fist to Rick's. "And you are quite likely the best fighter I have ever faced. I simply refuse to accept your resignation on any grounds." Frankly, he would do just about anything in his power to persuade the other agent to accept the position. Their bout had only cemented in his mind his confidence in his decision to make Rick McCoy his partner.

"Yeah, well, I think I'll hold off on that myself." A smile twisted the corner of Rick's mouth. "We might make a pretty formidable pair after all. I'm willing to look past the bizarreness to give our partnership a chance. To try anyway." His smile wavered. "It's going to be a bit of a challenge reevaluating a lot of what I thought was true."

"You would not be the first partner I have helped through that adjustment." Dante rested his hand on Rick's arm. "I will have your back in whatever way I can."

◇ ◇ ◇ ◇ ◇

A shower and a couple painkillers later, Rick joined Dante out in front of the complex. He shook his head when he saw the other agent. His face was paler than usual, but his hair and clothes were as perfect as always. Dante definitely didn't *look* like a man who could dish out the brutal beating he'd delivered only a few moments before. Rick started to shake his head, but stopped when it just made his head hurt more. He still had a lot of doubts and questions, but Dante's character and capabilities were no longer among them. Confidence in his partner would go a long way in covering all the other issues the job entailed.

He'd finally spoken with Gracie before he'd left for the gym. She'd been scared at his unresponsiveness, and angry that he'd scared her *before* he'd even broached the topic of his promotion and transfer. They'd argued. He asserted she always knew DC was the goal. She argued that if he was really serious about *them*, he'd have discussed it with her first. He couldn't begin to answer that without going into more detail about the last two days than he was prepared for, so they'd ended the conversation with an unresolved and shaky truce. Which might have explained his uncharacteristic brutality toward Dante in the match this morning.

They'd been assigned to break from the Zanotti case to canvas the area around the fountain where Dante had been shot. The sniper Rick had killed was still being identified, and all the meager evidence that had been collected immediately after the shooting was being processed. They didn't even have enough to go on to establish motive, or whether there was risk of another attempt on Dante's life. If they didn't want a repeat of the previous day, the shooting had to take priority.

Rick stopped on the front steps when he noticed Dante's car: a very well kept, white 1979 Pontiac Firebird with a bright red Phoenix on the hood and a red interior. Rick blew a low whistle. The car was gorgeous, and definitely what he should have expected Dante to drive.

"Don't tell me, you bought it new and have been driving it for the last forty years." Rick ran an appreciative hand over the polished white hood.

"It is quite fitting, no?" Dante smiled proudly.

"I have a question." Rick laughed. "What do you do if you have a case that requires that you *don't* draw attention to yourself?"

"That is precisely why I have you," Dante clapped him on the back with his left hand and rounded the car, still favoring his right side.

Rick frowned and hoped he hadn't actually injured his new partner. Watching Dante survive a headshot may have led him to forget that the other man could still be *hurt,* perhaps even badly. He opened his mouth to enquire after Dante's health, but never got the words out.

"Oh, hey, Dante!" A young man, probably in his early twenties, wearing worn brand name sweatpants and a tee shirt with a bigfoot framed by a stylized flaming phoenix dashed across the street toward them. A car slammed on both its brakes and its horn as he crossed carelessly in front of it. He looked Rick over critically. "You got a new partner."

"Agent McCoy, this is Paul Lynch." Contempt dripped from Dante's voice as he gestured a gloved hand at the young man.

"I host the viral YouTube channel 'Cryptid Conspiracies.'" Lynch offered his hand to Rick. "My screen name is VampirePhoenix. Maybe you've heard of me?" His grin widened at Dante. "Dante hates the nickname."

"I have told you repeatedly, *Paul,* that vampires are servants of darkness." Dante spoke with exaggerated patience, as if he was getting tired of explaining himself. "I am a servant of light, and find the association offensive."

"I find the contradiction hilarious." Lynch moved to clap Dante on the back, but Dante sidestepped to avoid him with a glare.

"Wait, you actually know about Dante?" Rick raised an eyebrow at the young man. Dante had made it sound like there weren't a lot of humans who knew about him, but it seemed to Rick that half of DC knew what Dante was.

"I've been following Dante for years. I know everything there is to know about him." Lynch rested a hand on the hood of Dante's car for a brief moment before Dante lifted it gingerly away and buffed out the fingerprints with his sleeve.

Rick caught the hero-worship in Lynch's eyes and the disgust in Dante's and wondered if *stalking* was a better term.

"You know, Dante, you could have made me your next partner." Lynch turned his back to Rick as he scolded Dante. "I know more about the mythic community than this guy could possibly know."

"It takes more than just a knowledge of mythics to be an effective partner," Dante responded quietly. He glanced over Lynch's shoulder at Rick apologetically. "Agent McCoy is a highly capable agent and exceeds all the requirements I expect from a partner."

"I'm taking criminology classes online, and I've studied every one of your cases." Lynch's voice rose in a whine. "I told you after Agent Azusa died that I was everything you needed."

"You've studied all *five hundred years* of his cases?" Rick asked skeptically. "I thought those files were classified."

"I have sources, Agent McCoy. If you're that experienced, you should understand that." Lynch turned on him with a venomous glare. "I also have all my followers tracking sightings of him around town. I've been at every case he's solved for the past three years. I can name his last twelve partners from memory. I was there when he had to kill Wes Azusa with his own hands." His voice rose as he stepped closer to Rick and stabbed him in the breastbone with his finger. "I'm more qualified than you. He should have chosen me."

Rick opened his mouth to respond, but Dante grabbed Lynch with one gloved hand and spun him around. Dante's other hand was bare and holding a fireball. His face was contorted in anger more intense than anything he'd shown with either of the mob bosses.

"You will apologize to Agent McCoy, immediately, *Paul.* No one lays a finger on my partner. If you knew me half as well as you claimed, you would know that at least." Dante snapped his fingers and the flame went out. "And I alone choose my partners according to strict qualifications based on centuries of experience. You do not meet those qualifications, and taking a couple classes won't change that." He released Lynch a bit roughly. "Go back to your online followers and be content that I tolerate your presence at all."

Lynch's face drained to white at Dante's anger, then flamed to purple at the demand that he apologize to Rick. He glared at Dante defiantly.

Dante sighed and pulled his glove back on. "Your century has a *wonderful* thing called a 'restraining order.' If you are going to continue to harass my partners and disrupt my work, I will secure one."

"I apologize for touching you and for thinking I'm a better partner for Dante than you are," Lynch said sullenly, his expression not conveying any apology at all.

"I accept your apology on the condition that you dial it back and stop stalking *my* partner." Rick showed his badge for emphasis. "You're going to get someone killed – quite possibly yourself or one of us. Try being a normal fan, not a psycho stan, and we can all get along nicely."

"'Psycho Stan.' Nice. Real mature." Lynch sneered, but returned the way he came, giving Rick an obscene gesture as soon as he was out of Dante's reach. "I'll still be here when you're done with him, Dante. You'll see. I can be the best partner you've ever had."

"I apologize." Dante shook his head as he climbed into the driver's seat. "Paul Lynch is –"

"Unstable? A stalker?" Rick got in the passenger's side and closed the door. "A psycho stan?"

"I don't know what that is." Dante laughed. "I was going to say 'persistent,' but any of those work as well. I would never take him to be my partner, even if he were the last human on earth."

"The restraining order might not be a bad idea." Rick pulled up the Cryptid Conspiracies channel on his phone. He curled his lip at all the Dante spotting videos, including the viral video of Dante's last partner's death, which he reported immediately. "Seriously, Dante, this guy is messed up."

"Hmm. I suppose." Dante frowned. "I try to avoid his videos, blog, him..."

"I don't blame you. He's got a problem." Rick reported another video of the inside of Dante's house when Dante wasn't home.

"Let's button up this case, and we'll see." Dante shrugged. "Interviews are boring, he'll likely leave me alone today."

Rick reported another offensive video, and just grunted. It didn't appear Lynch *ever* left Dante alone.

Chapter Seven

After a long and rather unproductive day, Rick woke to his phone ringing at five the next morning. This time it was Director Leon himself.

"You and Dante have another case." The director got to the point brusquely. "Male Caucasian, about thirty, works a dining cruise on the wharf. He was found floating beside the yacht he pilots this morning."

"If Dante's lead, why are you calling me?" Rick honestly didn't care who was lead, but he wasn't about to start stepping on the toes of a guy who could take a bullet to the head and walk away.

"Prelim report suggests a vampire got him."

"Ah." Rick threw off the covers and crossed to his dresser to start pulling out clothes. Dante's last partner had been taken by a vampire, supposedly. Whether Rick believed in all that or not, Dante clearly did, Which meant this case might be a bit triggering for him.

"He's going to try to cut you out. Don't let him," Director Leon warned. "Just watch your back and remember that the bullets in your gun are silver alloy, so if something goes for your throat, you have the stopping power to take it down."

"Seriously?" Rick paused and looked over at his gun sitting on his bed stand. These people really took this paranormal stuff seriously. "Just out of curiosity, what happens if Dante gets hit by a silver bullet? Is he dead-dead like your vampires and whatnot?" He couldn't deny what happened to Dante, but he couldn't explain it either. And it didn't mean he would just accept all the other weirdness as truth just because Dante existed.

"Ha. No." Director Leon barked a harsh laugh. "Nearly all of us have had to use our weapons on him at one point or another. The only thing that can keep Dante from resurrecting is to keep him from burning."

"Hold up. Why would I need to use my weapon on him?" A mental image of a flaming Dante coming at him while he pumped him full of silver-laced lead rose up in Rick's mind. He shook it off and swallowed hard. Dante didn't seem to be a monster. There had to be another explanation.

"Think about it, Rick." The director sighed. "When death is just a reset, there are a whole lot of things that are worse. Don't worry, it doesn't happen that often."

"You can't seriously be telling me that..." Rick trailed off. He'd only just started to accept that he'd have to watch his partner die repeatedly, the thought that he might have to kill his partner *himself* was about enough to send him back for the resignation paperwork. He rubbed his hands over his face. "Forget it. Just text me the info about the crime scene."

Rick drove to the address the director sent him. The MPD had done their jobs, and the area was cordoned off and a few uniformed officers kept the curious onlookers back from the crime scene.

"I'm looking for Agent Dante Brand. Fancy suit. Flaming red hair." Rick flashed his badge to the officer who appeared to be in charge.

"Yeah, we know Brand. He's on the boat with the victim." The officer looked him over. "You're his new partner?"

"Started yesterday." Rick wondered what other human officers thought of his new partner, so he added, "Do you work with him often?"

"On and off for twenty years." The officer shrugged. "He's always polite and efficient, but man, do they give him the weird cases. Like this one. The first responders swear it looks like a vampire got him. Can you believe that?"

"That's pretty unbelievable," Rick agreed dryly. "I'm sure there's a reasonable explanation. Maybe a serial killer with a Dracula fetish." He was an awful lot less sure than he'd been twenty-four hours earlier, and that bothered him just a bit. He ducked under the tape. "I probably should catch up to him before he does all the fun stuff and leaves me with the paperwork."

"Tell him Mallory said hi." The officer waved him through. "And, hey, if you ever find out what his skin care regimen is, let me know. I swear he looks even younger than the last time I saw him. I'd love to get my wife in on that."

Rick snorted as he walked away. The poor guy would be better off buying his wife some cream at the mall. He was pretty sure getting sniped wouldn't work out quite as well for her.

He found Dante onboard a sleek yacht with the name Potomac Siren painted on the side. He was standing on deck interviewing a woman with long blonde hair, a slender body, and a tear-streaked face. She wore a pale blue sundress, beaded sandals, and a necklace made from an elaborately painted cowrie shell. Dante looked up the moment Rick's foot first hit the gangplank. His face paled and his lips pulled into a tight line, then almost immediately melted into a forced smile.

"Ah, Ms. Johanna Bennett, this is my partner, Agent Rick McCoy." Dante gestured to Rick. "Rick, this is the victim's wife and the co-owner of this vessel."

"I'm sorry for your loss." Rick nodded to her solemnly.

"Thank you so much for your time, Ms. Bennett." Dante stepped back and rested a firm hand on Rick's arm. "I'll get my partner up to speed and let you know if I have any other questions."

The woman nodded as Dante steered Rick back toward the gangplank. "I'm glad you're here. I'm going to need help with this case."

"Huh. Okay." Rick narrowed his eyes and slowed up. Dante wasn't behaving at all like the director had implied he would, but he wasn't acting *right* either. "What are we looking at?"

"Chip Bennett – the victim – was closing up for the night last night and never came home. His wife – a mermaid, as you may have noticed –"

"And how would I have noticed that?" Rick interrupted. "She looked like she had legs to me."

"Yes. Apart from the fact that the merfolk are allied with the fishermen and boat crews, she wore a painted conch. The merfolk use enchanted shells to give them legs and allow them to live on land for longer periods of time." Dante waved a hand like he's just explained something basic, like where the President lived. "Her time was up, so she had to return to the sea last night and didn't realize he didn't come home." Dante lowered his voice. "She found him this morning on the flybridge deck with what appeared to be a bite mark on his neck. The medical examiner on the scene said it appears all his blood was drained."

"Vampires? In DC? Other than the ones in suits working at the Capitol?" Rick tried to joke, but Dante didn't seem to get it. His partner looked surprised for a moment, then realized he was teasing and shook his head.

"As hard as it is to believe, I think we probably should look into the possibility that there might be other murders like this in the area. Someone trying to make it look like a vampire murderer." Dante guided him further from the decks and closer to the parking lot. "We're almost wrapped up here. So I'd like you to get a head start checking on that. Contact the Capitol Police, Metro Police Department, Maryland State Police, Virginia State Police, probably the FBI wouldn't hurt, as well."

There it was, the busy paperwork distraction Rick had anticipated. Contacting all those departments would take at least the rest of the day, if not longer. "Doesn't PNI have a research specialist?"

"Yes," Dante drew out the word slowly, "but I know I can trust you to make sure nothing is missed."

"Are you sure it's not that you want me as far from this case as possible, preferably safely inside the office?" Rick turned and shook Dante's hand free. He still wasn't entirely comfortable with the flamethrowing agent touching him, gloves or no gloves.

"Of course not, you're a highly capable agent –"

"Who is fully capable of handling himself."

"So was Wes." Dante's voice was barely audible, but each word was a staccato punch. "I'll not lose another partner the same way."

"I'll have Director Leon buy me a silver studded dog collar and a bottle of garlic perfume. You're not going solo." Rick crossed his arms over his chest, hoping Dante didn't really demand he did either one. "Why would a vampire kill a yacht owner?"

"Because he had human blood? Not unlike you." Dante sounded irritated, but at least stopped pushing Rick toward the police line.

"You'll have to enlighten me sometime why you're so repulsive to them that you can just go off chasing after them without fear." Rick matched Dante's irritation with his own. Half of it was irritation at the whole ridiculousness of *vampires,* half with Dante's bull-headedness. "Unless this fantasy world of yours just plays by whatever rules you make up for it."

Dante drew back and stiffened. He muttered something in Italian or Latin that Rick couldn't decide if it was a prayer or a curse, then took a deep breath. "I can assure you that these 'rules' are deadly serious, and if you can't trust me far enough to accept that much, perhaps it would be better if you did return to the office."

"And if you can't trust me enough to handle myself when this stuff gets weird, maybe you should have picked a different partner to begin with," Rick snapped. "I'm sure VampirePhoenix is still available. *He* won't have any trouble accepting that basically every weird thing imaginable is *real.* Pardon me if twenty-four hours and a couple miraculous resurrections aren't quite enough to make me swallow everything without question."

Regret, disgust, and a little fear marched across Dante's expressive face in order before his expression settled on remorse. "I apologize, *mon ami*. You are right of course. I was expecting too much from you and not giving you enough credit at the same time. I just... had hoped neither of us would have to face this particular threat so soon. I fear neither of us are ready."

"Tch. We probably aren't, too bad the vampire didn't have the courtesy to ask before sucking the blood out of someone in our town." Rick's own anger cooled.

"They can be rude like that." Dante chuckled. "And, to answer your question, yes, I am repulsive to them. Vampires are creatures of darkness and evil. Fire both illuminates and purifies. My resurrection grace is in my blood, and they cannot tolerate it."

"So what is the next step? Preferably one that doesn't involve either of us going off alone, or garlic perfume." Rick was suddenly sharply aware they'd been fighting near a crime scene like an old married couple. Thankfully, Dante had managed to maneuver him far enough from the boat to avoid notice.

"His wife was quite adamant no one had any reason to want him dead, though of course I have the office double checking financials and such." Dante sighed and rounded his flashy car. "Which means we'll need to visit Laysha and inquire about her coven." He paused to open the driver's door. "You're *sure* I can't convince you to at least stay in the car?"

"No chance." Rick scoffed. "You're stuck with me."

Chapter Eight

Dante fingered the stainless steel combat rosary in his pocket nervously the whole way to City Center DC. Rick had insisted on driving, probably so Dante didn't attempt to ditch him again, which gave Dante too much time to revisit the last case he had worked with Wesley Azusa.

Wes, a self-proclaimed "holy roller" had adapted quickly to PNI and what Rick had referred to as 'weirdness.' He'd struggled more so with Dante's first resurrection a year and a half after they'd been paired together, accusing Dante of being possessed and attempting to perform an exorcism. The next time had occurred nearly three years later and their relationship was established well enough not to elicit the same extreme response. Still, Wes had never learned to accept Dante's nature and attempted to preserve Dante's life as passionately as if Dante had been a mere human.

That was the flaw in their partnership that had led to Wes's death. They'd tracked a rogue coven of vampires to a nightclub in Georgetown where they were luring college kids with promises of thrills and fun, then "proselytizing" them.

Dante's appearance was enough to allow him to go undercover as a freshman at Georgetown University with Wes operating as his handler. Dante had gotten a job as a salesman at the makeup counter at the department store Laysha worked for and had quickly drawn the attention of other vampires for his flawless style and easy grace.

"Dang, Dante. What are you wearing? It smells like you got caught in my middle school Sunday School class body spray war." Wes had teased when he'd picked Dante up from work. It'd been easier to age him up a bit to look like he could be Dante's dad than down to play the college kid.

"The resurrection fire in my blood is noxious to vampires. I needed to mask my scent." The cheap perfume was noxious to Dante, especially compared to the custom blend cologne he usually wore, as were the unwashed black jeans and turtleneck he'd borrowed from Charles's teenaged son, but for this to work he needed there to be no hint that he was anything other than a normal human college kid. He glared down at the fourth cup of crushed ice he'd eaten in the last hour to bring his core temperature closer to normal human range. "Deke invited me to The Black Bat Lounge to hang out with them tonight. I think this might be it."

"I don't like this at all. What if they figure you out? What if they *bite* you?" Wes's knuckles grew white as he tightened them on the steering wheel. "I told you I should have been the one undercover."

"If they discover me, the worst that can happen is I die, which they will regret more than I will. And there are far worse things than death, especially where vampires are concerned." Dante had reminded him. "Remember, the entire point of this operation is that we're trying to catch them turning a human. Me. Their bite can't hurt me, so your focus needs ro be on the case, and limiting collateral damage if they happen to get me down."

Wes had simply grunted his disagreement as he had parked at the all night diner down the street from the club. "I'll be here if you need me." He'd passed Dante an earwig microphone, then gone in to check out the all day breakfast menu.

Dante had walked to the club – a black painted brick building with no windows and gaudy signage with a heavy goth aesthetic. He curled his lip and hoped fervently the lack of windows simply hinted to the vampire goth motif and not a more lascivious occupation.

The interior was dimly lit and a mixture of vampires and humans dressed as vampires milled around the large, open area. He paid the cover charge and scanned the room for Deke or one of his other coworkers.

"Dan! You came!" Deke crossed to him with open arms. His coworker had changed from the khaki and polo uniform they wore at the mall, to black jeans, a black silk button-down shirt, and markedly *less* makeup than he wore to work. His face was pale and his blood red lips framed perfect and too-sharp teeth. He also wore too much cologne, to mask the smell of blood and decay inherent to vampires. "What do you think? Wild, right?"

"When you told me about this club, I was a little nervous, honestly." Dante skillfully masked his revulsion at the vampire's icy touch with feigned youthful awe. "It's really nothing like I expected."

"Come on, I'll introduce you to a few friends." Deke placed his arm across Dante's shoulders and led him to a group of people at the bar. Three were vampiresses – one that Dante recognized from the mall – and the last a human girl with a glazed expression. All five had glasses of what could have been a Bloody Mary. Or given the context, something else far less innocuous. "Dan, this is Elvira, Chiara, Chastity, and Ron. That's Molly."

"Mmm, Deke, is this the guy you've been telling us about?" The vampiress Deke had addressed as Elvira set her glass down and stood. She wore a cheap black dress that hugged her curves and exposed about as much as she could get away with publicly. She pressed her body to Dante's, rested her chin on his shoulder and reached her arm around to stroke his neck on his opposite side. "Surely a handsome young man like you isn't here alone."

"Uh, yeah. I'm currently single." Dante stammered a bit in what he hoped would be taken as the nerves of an inexperienced young man being courted by an older woman. Reality was that he was put off by the closeness of her fangs to his throat and the way she had begun toying with the collar of his shirt. He'd intentionally neglected to tell Wes that vampire bites made him violently ill, because it was better for him to be sick in bed for a week than for his human partner to be turned or killed. It still didn't make him look forward to receiving one.

"Well, we can take care of that, for tonight at least," she whispered in his ear, then caught the lobe lightly between her teeth. She pulled away from him and motioned to the bartender as the vampiress Deke had called Chiara stood and wrapped her arm around him on the other side. She wore black as well, but her dress was long and flowing, with an impossibly high slit up her left leg and a ridiculously low neckline.

"We're alone tonight, too." She giggled and pressed her blood red lips to his neck where his pulse throbbed beneath the skin.

Dante pulled back. This was going too fast, and far too openly for his liking. Once they realized what he was, everyone in the room was in danger. "Wow, you girls sure are friendly. I'm, uh, not sure I'm the kind of guy who goes that fast on a first date. Maybe we could get a couple drinks and get to know each other?"

"Exactly what I had in mind." Chastity moved over to make room for him at the bar, and set a glass identical to the others in front of him. "House special. I promise you'll be ready for anything after this."

That wasn't exactly an encouraging promise. Dante picked up the glass and sniffed it. In order to turn a human into a vampire, the human had to drink the blood of the vampire enslaving him, as well as being the vampire's victim. The strong-smelling beverage would be the easiest way to do that. He pretended to sip at the drink as he cast a sideways glance at the human girl Molly. Ron and Deke were paying her the same kind of attention the vampiresses were paying Dante, but she was already lethargic and her glass was nearly empty.

Elvira, Chiara, and Chastity were all looking at him expectantly, clearly waiting for him to actually finish the drink. Bile rose in Dante's throat and he barely managed to swallow it down. He'd never actually had to *drink* vampire blood before, but he was pretty certain he wasn't going to react well to it. *Lord Jesus Christ, holy Son of God, may the virtue that you have blessed me with cover even this.* He knocked back the revolting drink, slammed the glass back on the counter, and grinned at them ridiculously.

His stupid grin froze on his face as he recognized the man sitting at the booth across the lounge from them. Wes sat with a matching glass in hand as he chatted up a vampiress dressed like a waitress. Pain clenched Dante's stomach, whether from the foul drink he'd just downed or the fear for his partner was impossible to tell. *Wes, you fool. I say things for a reason.*

For a brief moment, Dante's attention was diverted from the group he was with as he desperately racked his brain for a way to eject his partner from the club without exposing himself, sacrificing the case, and placing Wes in even more danger. His distraction was taken as submission, and sharp teeth piercing his carotid artery snapped him back to focus with a shout.

Elvira pulled back immediately, grabbing at her mouth as she fell to her knees with a scream of agony. Dante winced as he pressed a hand to his neck. The wound itself was inconsequential, but the combined venom from the bite and the vampire blood he ingested would make him worthless to defend the innocents around him in a few short moments if he didn't clear the room.

Deke rushed to her side and tilted her face up to look at her. "Her mouth and throat are burned." Anger contorted his face as he stood and advanced on Dante. "What kind of demon are you?"

With a sigh, Dante made the sign of the cross and pulled his gloves free. "I am not a demon. I am opposite of you in every possible way. You and this establishment are in violation of the Mythic Code of Conduct. You must all answer to the Council for your crimes."

"You're that phoenix, Brand." Deke swore colorfully. "I can't believe I thought you were my friend."

"You brought me here to turn me into a vile creature and had your coven attack me. I am not the one who violated our 'friendship.'" Dante scoffed. The nausea from the toxic drink was becoming unbearable and searing pain spread outward from the bite. He raised his voice. "Wes, clear the room!"

Wes didn't move.

Deke, Ron, and the vampiresses did. They attacked Dante as one, clawing at him and attacking him with whatever weapons they could find. Elvira came at him with a butcher knife, but Dante caught her by the wrist and burned her to ash before she could land the blow. That cleared the room as effectively as if Wes had done his job. Dante would have been worried about his partner, but Ron picked up a barstool and hit Dante hard enough to drive him to his hands and knees. Dante held one arm to his stomach as the vampires piled on him. Wes would have to fend for himself.

He resurrected with a gasp, scrambling like always to gather his scattered thoughts. He'd died, clearly. How was unclear. Where was his partner? The intense heat from his resurrection fire had left a ring of ash, what appeared to be human remains, and spreading flames within the room where he stood. He couldn't remember the last time he saw Wes, and what little remained of the bodies was burned beyond recognition. *Lord Jesus, please grant Wes survived the blast.* Still, the fact that Wes was nowhere to be seen didn't bode well for his partner's survival.

Dante bent to pick up his gloves from the ash, irritated that Wes wasn't around to give him something to wear, while desperately hoping his partner survived so he could yell at him. He was halfway up when someone hit him hard enough to knock him on his back. Dante instinctively pulled his bare hands up and away so he didn't incinerate his attacker before he could assess the situation.

"Wes? What are you–" Dante broke off with an angry cry. The man on top of him wore Wes's clothes, but his blood red lips stood out from his white face and his teeth were unnaturally sharp.

"God have mercy." Dante groaned as grief and deep horror gripped him. "Wes! For heaven's sake, man, stop." Perhaps it was not too late. Perhaps his friend had not fully turned.

Wes had grabbed him by the shoulders and gone for his throat.

With a sharp gasp, Dante shook off the terrible flashback. His hands trembled and the metal beads of his rosary bit into his palm in spite of his glove. He'd hadn't had a choice. Sometime between when he'd seen Wes at the table and when he'd resurrected, the vampires had taken Wes out of revenge. He tried to tell himself that the Wes he'd known was already gone, or that it was Wes's fault for not following protocol, but the truth was that Wes had been there to back him up, had been taken for the sole reason of punishing Dante, and had ultimately been burned to ash by Dante's own hand. Rick's face replaced Wes's in Dante's mind's eye, and Dante bit back a low sob. He couldn't handle it if it happened again.

"I'm sorry." Rick's voice broke his reverie. "I hadn't considered how difficult this would be for you. Not that it means I'm heading back to the office," his partner added hastily, "just that I'm sorry for hassling you about it."

"Wes mistrusted me and my 'rules.'" Dante quietly tucked the rosary back into his pocket. "If you are going in with me, I need to know that you trust me even when you don't understand or believe what I tell you."

"I don't understand ninety percent of what's happened since I walked into the director's office, and believe even less than that." Rick barked a sharp laugh. "But I have seen for myself that you're a capable agent, and I can trust you. Just remember, you're not the only one who lost a partner recently. You're not going solo and I will have your back, no matter how dangerous you think it is. Vampires, werewolves, or jackalopes, we face them together. Those are my terms, got it?"

"Those terms are acceptable." Dante grinned as he pointed to an empty parking spot near the mall entrance. "But, Rick, jackalopes aren't real."

"Oh, come on!"

Chapter Nine

*L*ord, what have I gotten myself into? Rick found himself praying for probably the hundredth time since watching Dante get sniped twenty four hours ago. Resurrecting phoenix humans were bad enough, but somehow Dante being one of the good guys made it easier to take. Vampires, though? Dante was scared enough Rick was nearly convinced they were real himself. Did that mean that whole thing yesterday about the dogs meant actual werewolves as well? What other things he'd written off as fantasy were actually real? And, really, were any of them worse than vampires?

Fear thou not; for I am with thee: be not dismayed; for I am thy God: I will strengthen thee; yea, I will help thee; yea, I will uphold thee with the right hand of my righteousness. A verse of Scripture came to mind, both applicable and encouraging in the face of all the uncertainty and weirdness. God was the one constant he could lean on regardless of what turned out to be real.

He followed Dante into the mall to an upscale department store. Not exactly the place he expected to find a nest – er – coven of vampires.

"Laysha is the Queen of the Vampires." Dante stopped outside the store and lowered his voice. "She has no love for me, but as the Vampire representative of the Mythic Council has no choice but to cooperate. She is no threat to either of us here."

"Vampires working the makeup counter at the mall? Not lawyers or politicians?" Rick teased. The mermaid at the wharf and the werewolf enforcers made more sense than this.

"Vampires are above all else manipulators who like to take advantage of their victims to get what they want. So they are well suited to sales. Plus, they are exceedingly vain."

Rick snorted at the hypocrisy of *Dante* calling someone vain.

Dante gave him a withering look and went on. "The Vampire Guild is aligned with cosmetology, sales, and some... less savory occupations. We are fortunate Laysha prefers an easily accessible trade."

They entered in front of the makeup counters and an impeccably dressed woman about Rick's age crossed to them with a wide grin. A grin that faded when she saw Dante.

"Oh. What do you want?" Her perfectly made up face contorted in disdain.

"Official business, Laysha." Dante showed her his PNI badge for emphasis. "One of yours took a sailor down by the wharf. I need to know if you've heard anything."

"No. My people have been lying low since the last scandal." She gave Rick a pitying look. "We have a bad enough reputation with the humans as it is."

She stepped closer to Rick and traced a long, painted nail along his scruffy jawline. "Is this your new one? I must say, he's better looking than your last one."

"Don't touch him, Laysha." Dante's volume didn't change, but the threat contained in his tone was undeniable.

"Pah. Keep your human pet, Dante." Laysha sniffed. "If owning just one of them soothes your conscience about selling yourself to the whole of humankind."

"Wait just a minute. We're partners." Rick bristled. At least the werewolf enforcer played the coded game with Dante. Laysha didn't seem to care if her disdain for humans was public knowledge. "No one owns anyone."

"Really? You *are* human, right? I can smell it in your blood. That makes you a lesser creature. Don't worry, it's not an insult. Many mythics keep your kind like you keep dogs. Even vampires do it." She smiled and bared her teeth at him. "As for Dante, what would you feel if a human played enforcer for a feral cat colony? Respect? Appreciation? Mythics can handle ourselves. We don't need Dante or PNI."

"Mythics need me and PNI if they wish to continue to live in harmony with the humans." Dante moved slightly so that he was between Laysha and Rick. "Mythic crimes can be handled by the Guilds until they involve humans. PNI makes sure that we maintain peace between the races."

"Maybe some of us think the price for harmony is too high," Laysha snapped. She waved a dismissive hand. "I'll ask around. It *is* in our best interest to make sure that a rogue isn't going around murdering the pets of other mythics. Mermaids can be quite vindictive."

"I'm sure the Council appreciates your enthusiastic cooperation." Dante nodded sarcastically and turned to go.

"She was quite blunt, wasn't she?" Rick scrambled after Dante. "Do all Mythics feel the same about humans?"

"No, most are quite happy to live as equals in harmony. Otherwise, we'd have had a devastating mythic-human war centuries ago." Dante gestured back at the department store entrance. "Vampires have always seen humans as little more than cattle, and of course resent having to subject their natural desires for peace. The other Mythic Guilds tend to see their relationships with the humans as mutually beneficial, and appreciate my role in keeping violations of the peace in check." He shrugged. "Until I come knocking on *their* door. It is the same way with human cops, no? Enforcement is appreciated until it touches them."

"I suppose." Rick frowned. He'd worked with officers who'd gone back to police the difficult neighborhoods they'd grown up in and had faced the same mixed response. Sell-out and traitor were some of the nicer things they'd been called as well. "Are there other Mythic officers in PNI?"

"A few, yes, mostly as liaisons to neighborhoods populated with their people. Intra-Guild crime is handled by the head of the guild – Laysha in this case. Inter-Guild crime is handled between the respective heads, or taken to the Council." He paused to get in the car. "My department handles capital crimes perpetrated by mythics on humans. Essentially, the crimes that would threaten human-mythic relations if they became public."

Rick thought about that for a moment as he started the car. "Is that why you insist your partner be human, to help broker human relations? I mean, you wouldn't need to worry about losing an immortal partner."

"Among other reasons." Dante fingered the embroidery on the hem of his glove. "For over a century after I was cursed, I was rejected by both man and mythics, without a guild and clearly not human. A human named Leonardo De Vinci saw my potential and eventually helped me get a job as the paranormal investigator to the King of France. Both sides see me as a tool. Mythics who know my history are prone to see me as 'just a bird', while humans are more likely to eventually appreciate me as a friend."

Rick considered commenting on the sadness of that observation, but was interrupted by the sound of classical music coming from Dante's pocket.

Dante pulled out his phone and answered, "Charles." He listened for a moment, tapped the speaker on, and turned the phone so they could both listen.

"We're still tracing the sniper Rick took out. He's *someone's* werewolf enforcer, but no one's claiming him at the moment, and he's not in our files."

The lack of progress in the investigation into an attempt on a federal agent's life – *his partner's life* – irked Rick to no end. He flashed Dante a look, but Dante was focused on the phone screen and showed no indication he was as irritated.

"That's not really why I called, though. Have you seen Lynch's most recent post?"

"More recent than the ones I reported after our run-in with him?" Rick snorted.

"Probably. It went viral an hour ago."

Rick called up the channel on his phone and saw the latest upload titled, "Mythic Murders Sweep DC."

"Holy God, Holy Mighty One, Holy Immortal One," Dante breathed under his breath. He snatched the phone from Rick's hands and pressed play. "Have mercy upon us and on the whole world."

"Amen," Rick added. Even with his limited knowledge, he knew this was like striking a match near a gas leak.

"That's right, Cryptid Conspiracies fans, VampirePhoenix has conclusive proof that a wave of murders are sweeping the city. Werewolves, Vampires, and other Mythics are rising up against humans in a bold way we've never seen before."

Pictures and video clips followed of the last two cases, narrated by Lynch's bombastic commentary declaring that the mythics were after every man and woman in the DC area.

"Vikas called," the director informed them grimly. "The Council is understandably concerned. They want our assurances that we're handling the PR on this. Obviously, we're trying, but it would be easier if we *solved* these cases."

"Do you think they're connected?" Rick asked skeptically. There had been zero similarity between the cases, at least on the surface. But what did he know? He hadn't even believed in vampires fifteen minutes ago.

"Honestly, no." Director Leon sighed. "But now that Lynch has opened that Pandora's Box, it's our responsibility to close it. We've got our research specialists working on tracking any overlaps the victims might have. I need you two to go back and interview the families and keep an eye out for anything that sounds similar."

"We will interview Ms. Zanotti's family immediately." Dante handed Rick back his phone. "I will eventually have to speak to Vikas myself as well."

"Do that. He tends to respond better to you than me." The director scoffed. "Remember the time we managed to get him a meeting with the President. *That* went well."

"I will speak to him," Dante assured the director softly. "Keep us informed if anything changes."

"You do the same. And, Rick, sorry about your baptism by fire." The director chuckled. "No pun intended, but it's not usually this intense the first week. Just remember you can call me at any time, for literally any reason."

"I'll remember." Honestly, though, everything was happening so fast Rick wasn't sure *what* to ask.

Dante tapped the screen and went back to a private conversation. He listened for a moment, frowned at Rick, started to protest, listened a bit more, said, "If you think that's necessary, Charles," then hung up.

"Yeah, that didn't sound ominous at all." Rick laughed a bit nervously.

"Nothing all that bad," Dante chuckled. "Charles has agreed to pick up the tab for our friendly wager. Text him the name of the restaurant of your choice and we'll go tonight."

"Since I *clearly* lost that 'friendly wager,' your concession doesn't make me feel much better." Rick folded his arms over his chest. "And certainly wouldn't elicit an 'if you think that's necessary' response."

"Charles is concerned that *this* might be too much for your first case. Werewolves, vampires, and *two* resurrections – not to mention the prospect of rising mythic-human tensions – all in your first week?" Dante shrugged, but looked at Rick sharply. "Traditionally, the current director, I, and my new partner meet for an evaluation after a month. Charles wants it tonight."

"And if I fail, what happens?" Rick narrowed his eyes. He couldn't possibly figure out how he could pass a monthly evaluation after two days.

"Charles would give you reduced responsibilities until the case is closed." Dante lowered his voice, "If you were still interested in the position after the evaluation, that is."

"That bad?"

"Usually the conversation is geared toward addressing concerns about difficulties adjusting to the rather... unexpected requirements of the job. You've not had time to adjust to the fundamental basics of the job, much less the discussions of the more complicated scenarios."

"Like shooting you myself?"

"Like that, yes. Among other things," Dante replied dryly. "Charles wants to make certain you're ready to face what may well be the most difficult case of the last fifty years."

"And if he sidelines me, who has your back in this 'most difficult case'?" Rick also wondered what kind of case fifty years ago might have been more difficult than the threat of paranormal warfare, but decided to focus on the problem at hand.

Dante didn't answer.

"Dante?" Would they truly rather sideline him and leave Dante without backup?

"I'm certain Charles would figure something out." He grinned at Rick. "You will simply have to pass the evaluation, no?"

Not happening. Rick glared at the steering wheel. He wasn't going to lie, and there was no way either Dante or Director Leon would take his honest answers for anything other than exactly what they were: an indication that he was in way over his head. "Where does Amara Zanotti's family live? This case isn't going to solve itself."

Dante accepted his change of subject with a nod and gave him an address.

Rick threw the car into gear and drove in uncomfortable silence to the home. As many times as he had considered quitting, the idea of being sidelined or fired didn't sit well with him. He mentally rehearsed his answers to the questions he knew were coming. If this was going to be his last opportunity to make a good impression for a while, he wanted it to be a good one. He wanted to make sure he ended his pending hiatus on his own terms.

Chapter Ten

Dante found Rick's silence on the ride disconcerting. If his new partner gave up now – or worse, took offense at the evaluation and quit – Dante would be quite irritated with Charles. His former partner blamed himself for Wes's death as much as Dante did, but no amount of insistence on Dante's part could convince the director that it was affecting his decision making. It had taken them eight months to agree on Rick McCoy as a replacement, and even that was with significant reluctance on Charles's part. Rick was adapting quicker than average, quicker than Charles himself had, but that meant nothing to Charles beyond the fact that Rick wasn't field tested yet. Dante suspected Charles would even rather sideline both Rick and Dante than risk a repeat of Wes or Gilles.

They pulled into the Silver Spring neighborhood where Amara Zanotti's parents lived, only to see several people gathered on the front lawn. Dante groaned. Joey Vizzini and Giuceppe Ciccarelli were flanked by half a dozen werewolf enforcers, nearly nose to nose as they screamed at each other.

"If you say a word about me staying in the car I will punch you myself." Rick didn't even look at Dante as he parked in the street in front of the house and opened his door.

"Your werewolf killed her, Giuceppe, because you were jealous." Joey's face was red and his eyes were bright with tears.

"If I was jealous enough to kill, I'd'a killed you rather than her, you glorified gigolo." Ciccarelli pushed Vizzini back with his hands on his shoulders, causing the trio of men standing behind Vizzini to step forward threateningly.

Dante stepped between the feuding groups, placed a gloved hand on the chest of each of the young men, and pushed them apart.

"Mind your own business, Brand." Vizzini shoved him instead. "Me and my boys are gonna make this murdering scumbag pay."

"Ciccarelli and Wharton's alibi is being checked." Dante brushed invisible dirt from his lapels where Vizzini had touched him. "This isn't going to help anyone."

"I don't agree." Vizzini motioned to the men behind him. "Ordering my dogs to take out those two will help a lot of people."

At the word "dogs," all three of the men behind him started to transform into werewolves.

"Your dogs will have to get through ours first." Wharton snarled as the three men flanking him followed.

◈

When the first enforcer turned into a wolf, Rick's hand went for his gun immediately – a trembling hand, with his feet rooted in place by sheer will. The man's face contorted into a muzzle and fangs while his hands and feet turned into clawed paws. His partner followed suit, leaving Joey and Wharton flanked by snarling wolves in the remains of human clothing.

Giuceppe swore loudly. "I have my own, Joey. You can't make accusations like that and get away with it." He snapped his fingers, and the three enforcers behind him turned into wolves as well.

Rick's legs felt weak. He'd convinced himself that all Dante's talk about 'dogs' had just been trained attack dogs, but the reality of werewolves stood right in front of him. The director's threat to sideline him rang in the background of his brain. If he passed out now, he may as well skip the evaluation dinner and go straight to IKEA for a comfortable desk chair. He gritted his teeth, spread his legs, and took his gun in both hands. *Lord, help me stand even when I don't understand.*

I will uphold thee with the right hand of my righteousness.

"Vizzini, Ciccarelli, order your dogs to stand down before I arrest both of you." Dante threatened mildly, clearly not fazed by the men who turned into animals right next to him.

"Butt out, Bird Brain," Ciccarelli snapped. "Nobody asked for your involvement. Ciccarellis can handle themselves."

"Yeah, Vizzinis, too." Vizzini echoed. "We have this handled. Back off."

"I will not ask again." Dante started to pull his fingers free of his right glove.

"You won't get the chance." Wharton pointed at Dante. "Anthony, Jethro, David, take him out, then get his partner!"

Three werewolves lunged at Dante, knocking him off his feet before he could get his gloves off.

For a moment, Rick froze, his normal training to avoid hitting the victim taking the fore. Then he remembered the wounds on Zanotti's body and Dante's resurrections earlier. His partner was dead if he *didn't* take the shot, and would resurrect even if he missed.

He hoped. *Lord, make him resurrect.* Praying for something he'd have sworn was theologically impossible a week ago made him *very* uncomfortable, but nothing about this whole thing made him comfortable.

Dante wasn't moving, and the wound in his throat clearly was the reason why. With Dante dead, the werewolves turned their attention to Rick.

"Forget the human. Tear out the phoenix's heart." Wharton roared. "Let's see him resurrect then."

Rick snapped off three shots, anger at Wharton's command overriding his uncertainty. All three wolves fell.

"Nico, Leroy, and Tim, take care of the phoenix before he can resurrect!" Wharton screamed at Vizzini's werewolves. "The human is—"

Furious at Wharton's orders, and the upending of his own reality, Rick punched him in the face before he got out another word.

Wharton staggered back in shock, his hands clutching his bleeding nose.

Rick aimed his gun at the remaining werewolves as he pulled his cuffs out for Wharton. "Heel, or I'll end you all."

The trio whimpered, laid their heads on their front paws, and tucked their tails between their legs as Dante's resurrection fire illuminated the whole yard.

"You two idiots sit down with your hands behind your heads." Rick gestured with his gun at the two feuding lovers. Satisfied that Dante was at no risk of dying again, Rick grabbed Wharton by the arms and started to read him his rights.

◇

Dante resurrected with a gasp, scrambling to collect his situational awareness to protect himself and his partner. *Werewolves.* He grimly realized that Charles had gotten Rick his trial after all.

"You have the right to remain silent." Rick was reading Wharton his rights as he harshly pulled the enforcer's arms behind his back and cuffed him. Blood streamed from Wharton's nose and a dark circle ringed his left eye.

Pushing aside his concern about his lack of clothes, Dante scooped up his gloves and scanned the yard. Vizzini and Ciccarelli sat in the grass, fingers woven behind their heads, glaring at each other. Three inert masses of singed fur lay at the edge of his resurrection circle, and the three remaining werewolves lay on their front paws in submission at Rick's feet. Dante knelt to examine the nearest body. Surely Wharton's pack wasn't so foolish as to stay in his resurrection radius long enough to be killed. All three had bullet wounds to the brain.

He sat back on his heels and laughed.

"What's so funny?" Rick glared at him as he shoved Wharton into the back of his SUV.

"Charles need not have worried so much. Anyone who can take out three werewolves with one shot each, subdue three more, and arrest their alpha – all before I resurrect – is more than qualified for the job." Dante looked down at himself in chagrin. "Speaking of the job..."

His bag hit him in the side before he could finish.

"Hm. Thank you." Dante quickly began to dress, acutely aware that the Zanottis and their neighbors were beginning to stare curiously at the scene. As he buttoned his pants, he looked his partner over critically. "You are unharmed? How did you manage that? Wharton is not an easy foe."

"I... may have punched him in the face while he was freaking out about me shooting his dogs." Rick rubbed the back of his neck as his face grew red. "He ordered his pack to tear out your heart to see if you could resurrect without it. I took out the dogs, then punched him in the face when he ordered the other three to fulfill his order before you woke."

Dante laughed. "I told you I chose you because I needed someone willing to punch a mythic in the nose for killing me. You didn't believe me."

"I still don't believe any of this." Rick grumbled. "I'm calling for backup to take care of these morons. You finish getting dressed so we can interview the family."

Dante shook his head with a grin as he shrugged on his shirt. He was feeling much better about Rick's evaluation tonight.

Chapter Eleven

The interview was pretty unhelpful. Amara Zanotti's parents, freaked out by the scene on their lawn, refused to let Dante in the house, mostly blamed all the "monsters" they'd just seen for their daughter's death, and praised Rick profusely for his bravery. Even Rick's best attempts to convince them that answering his questions would help button up the case against her murderers, yielded nothing but more bile for both Vizzini and Ciccarelli.

"And now you see why I simply must have a human partner." Dante shrugged when Rick reported back to him at the car. He'd finished helping the other agents load the werewolves and their partners into the squad car and now simply leaned against Rick's Jeep waiting for him. "Humans are much less cooperative once they find out what I am."

"They weren't that much more cooperative for me, honestly." Rick climbed into the driver's seat with a grunt. "Hopefully PNI's researchers have better luck looking for a connection."

"Hm. We can check after lunch." Dante slid into the seat next to him with noticeably less concern about the state of his car. "My treat."

"Shouldn't it be my treat?" Rick struggled to keep his turgid emotions from his voice, but failed. "I lost our friendly wager quite miserably, broke the record for fastest back to back resurrections, and probably broke the record for most resurrections in a twenty-four hour period."

"Not even close."

"I really don't want to know," Rick snapped. If he had to hear one more story about vampires or yeti or the Loch Ness Monster, he'd lose it. "The point is, we both know I'm failing that evaluation tonight, and the least I can do before I'm reassigned to a position as desk jockey is buy you lunch."

"We both know that, do we?" Dante chuckled softly.

"Have you ever had a partner shoot you for being infuriating?" Rick glared at his partner and decided he was glad they weren't moving yet. He narrowly avoided another biting comment about Dante's divergent reality and settled for, "How can it possibly go any other way? I couldn't even keep those werewolves from tearing out your throat."

"Ah, but you kept your nerve, took them out, assured my safe resurrection, and have not collapsed into a nervous fit."

"Yet." Rick made a face. The quietness of his hotel room seemed both welcoming and intimidating. *Lord, help me to lean on You.*

"Yet," Dante agreed softly. "Charles – and I – are above all concerned that you can come through in the clinch, when everything you thought you know is turned upside down and your very soul rebels against what every sense tells you is true. This is what you did today. Charles will have questions, and he will want to make sure any you have are answered, but I do not anticipate any trouble. Not after your performance today."

Rick fell silent. He was too overwhelmed to have any tangible questions.

"Can we swing by my hotel first at any rate?" He finally asked, tugging at the center of his polo shirt with his left hand. "Wharton's blood is all over my shirt, and I don't have a change of clothes in the trunk."

"Certainly." Dante graciously accepted his change in topic with a wave of his gloved hand. "There's a truck that sells the best carnitas within walking distance of your hotel. You may change while I pick up lunch."

Rick showered and changed quickly, then headed back down to wait for Dante. It was a beautiful day and the hotel had a beautifully landscaped front lawn. He went out the front door and walked along the sidewalk in the general direction Dante had disappeared. He wasn't as convinced as Dante was that tonight's meeting would go well and the fresh air made him feel less likely to 'lose his nerve.' He pulled his phone out of his pocket to text Dante his location. Anything to keep from having even a moment to think about things before tonight.

"You Agent Rick McCoy of PNI?" A gruff voice spoke from the shadows at the entrance to the parking garage.

Rick froze, one hand on the butt of his gun, the other holding his thumb over the quick dial icon to call Dante. The fact that they called him out for working for PNI, indicated this was going to get over his head fast. *If I'm going to keep facing mythic beings, I'm going to need a mythic weapon.* "Depends. If you're here about the gas bill, the check's in the mail."

"Funny. You're going to give your partner a message for us." The owner of the voice stepped into the light. He looked like a goblin that went to a Macys half price sale. His face was squashed and distorted, and his pointed ears were twice the size of a human's. His clothes were expensive, but mismatched, and not nearly as fine as Dante's.

"I'll give you his phone number and you can call him yourself. I'm a federal agent, not a process facilitator." Rick tried to take a step back into the street, but another ill-dressed creature blocked him off.

"I'm afraid my boss decided he needs a bit more dramatic example." The goblin pulled a mid-length blade from beneath his jacket. Rick didn't know a whole lot about goblin weapons, but the fancy damascus steel dagger was not what he expected.

"Look, I don't know your boss, or his beef with my partner, but I'm sure we can talk this through." Rick turned so his back was against the wall and he wasn't risking getting anything stuck in his back. He raised the phone as he tapped Dante's number. "Let me just get Dante here, you get your boss here, and we can all–"

The goblin that had blocked him in swiped at his arm with another fancy dagger. Rick pulled his arm back, and drew his gun, but the motion exposed his left side. He fired twice at the attacking goblin as the lead goblin lunged to his open side. He twisted quickly to fire at the remaining goblin, but didn't move far enough fast enough. The dagger thrust caught his side beneath his arm, and slipped between his ribs. Fire spread through his chest, and he dropped to one knee. His phone and his gun clattered to the pavement, as he struggled to breathe.

"Rick?" Dante's voice sounded far away coming from the phone.

The goblin kicked the phone away, pushed the dagger in deeper, then pulled it free and dropped it where the phone had been. He crouched in front of Rick and sneered.

"I think Dante will get our message loud and clear."

◇◇◇◇◇

Dante's phone rang just as he paid the food truck vendor. Notes from the final movement of Stravinsky's Firebird rose persistently from his pocket while he juggled the styrofoam containers of beef carnitas to get a free hand. He fished the phone out of his pocket and answered. "Rick?"

A strangled cry and the sound of the phone clattering to the ground was the only response.

"Rick!" Dante dropped their dinner where he stood and dashed back to Rick's apartment. All mythics had enhanced speed, strength, and stamina, but at this moment Dante would have given the rest of his lives to be able to fly. *God, grant me speed and please spare my partner's life.*

He pulled up short at the hotel. Had someone been waiting for Rick inside? Had he even made it into the building? The wrong choice on where to seek Rick first could cost his partner his life. *God, guide me...*

Was that blood? Dante's heart shuddered. Bloody footprints lead out from the parking garage beside the building. As cautiously as he dared, Dante approached the dim parking garage, pulling his fingers free from his right glove as he went. The footprints grew darker as they led further into the lowest level, where they stopped at a familiar body lying in a pool of fresh blood behind a cement pillar.

"Merciful God, not again. Please, not so soon." Dante's voice caught in anguish as he knelt beside his partner. A deep, jagged stab wound in his side still pulsed with blood. He was alive, but would not be for long at this rate.

Let us therefore approach the throne of grace with boldness, so that we may receive mercy and find grace to help in time of need.

Dante had never been one to lack boldness, and he wasn't about to change that with his partner's life on the line.

Merciful, Gracious God, help me be in time. Grant me Rick's life. Taking care not to add burns to his friend's injuries, Dante cleared the blood-soaked clothing from the wound and quickly cauterized it. Rick barely responded to the searing pain.

To be with Me is far better. A verse of Scripture softly touched his mind.

Dante's blood ran cold. *But for him to remain in the flesh is more necessary for me. Please, Lord, forgive my selfishness. I can't do this again. Not so soon.*

The rest of the passage touched his heart, carrying with it a flood of peace, *"Since I am convinced of this, I know that I will remain and continue with all of you for your progress and joy in faith."* Paul had been speaking of himself, but Dante held that verse in faith, trusting that God would allow Rick to continue with him.

Dante was neither a doctor nor a healer, but he knew getting the bleeding stopped was half the battle. He dialed 911 on his phone while he shrugged out of his jacket to use as a blanket to cover Rick while he waited for emergency services to arrive. It was then his eyes rested on a bloodied elfin blade. Rage contorted his face. If Rick died today, the elf-kind would have much to answer for.

Vengeance is mine, I will repay. The soft voice of the Holy Spirit reminded him.

The line between vengeance and justice was often blurred in his experience. Rick *would* get justice, and by God's grace, Dante would avoid falling into vengeance as he sought justice for his friend.

Chapter Twelve

Dante called Charles to meet the ambulance at the hospital, then went to his own brownstone to change immediately. Rick's blood soaked his pants where he had knelt beside him, his coat where he had laid it over Rick's body, and his gloves where he had tended Rick's wound. The stains were bad enough, but the fact that it was his partner's blood made him want to burn everything. Every spot was like an accusation to his failure. How could he have let this happen? If he'd been with Rick, he could have protected him. He could have negotiated with the assassin. He had to have been the target, after all. Rick hadn't been his partner long enough to tick off the mythics on his own. It should have been him. He bagged the bloody clothes to go to the dry cleaner, but he had to wash the gloves himself. Scrubbing them in the sink felt like washing his hands of Rick's blood.

Finally satisfied that the last shadow of pink was gone from his gloves, Dante dried his hands, dressed in a navy double breasted bespoke suit with a scarlet silk shirt, and prepared to face Elayna, the elf queen. He could do nothing for Rick, and whether his partner lived or died, someone needed to be held accountable for his attack.

The elves were aligned with the bakers and restaurateurs, and their queen ran one of the most prestigious cake bakeries in town.

Dante entered the bakery and strode confidently to the counter.

"Can I help you, sir?" A young woman in a pink apron finished checking out the customer in front of him and smiled.

"I need to speak with Elayna Essenfay." Dante kept his voice soft and tried not to be intimidating. The girl was not an obstacle or a threat.

Her smile wavered. "I'm sorry, but Ms. Elayna is very busy today."

"Tell her Dante Brand insists."

The girl frowned, but went to the back anyway. She returned and shook her head. "You'll have to come back later–"

Dante calmly removed his left glove and rested his hand on a tiered display cake, leaving a pile of ash on the counter. His voice was still soft and calm when he replied, "I will not leave until I speak to her. Try again."

The girl scuttled away again, this time returning with a thin gray haired woman with anger in her eyes.

"That cake was worth nearly a hundred dollars. What's the matter with you?" She put her hands on her hips and snapped at him.

"One of your people attacked my partner this morning." Dante picked up a napkin in his bare hand and watched it burn like flash paper before continuing. "If he dies, I will be burning much more than a cake."

"Attacked *your* partner? No one's that stupid." The elf queen scoffed, but fear lurked in her eyes. The girl looked terrified.

"Someone was." Dante remembered the blood running down the drain as he'd tried to wash his gloves and squeezed his eyes closed. "Someone will answer to me."

"Annika, close the shop and go home." Elayna gestured to the girl. "Dante and I need to talk."

"Ma'am?" The girl stammered, she looked at the ashes Dante had left behind. "Are you sure I shouldn't call the police?"

"He's with the police, darling. He's not going to hurt me." The elf queen gently pushed her to the door and turned the sign to "closed." She turned to face Dante. "You do realize I could bring the full force of the elven people on you for threatening me like this."

"A pair of assassins attacked my partner today. They stabbed him with an elven blade and left him for dead." Dante pulled his glove back on and looked her in the eye. "Swear to me it was not one of yours and

I will pay for the cake. Lie to me, and I will come back and burn the whole shop."

"Sneaking around assassinating the human allies of our enemies is not our style, even if I did count you as an enemy, which I don't." She crossed her arms over her chest and frowned. "And burning things like a vengeful pyromaniac isn't usually your style either. Grief has clouded your judgment."

"He would have bled out if I had been a block further away when he called. Someone wanted him dead, either to distract me or to warn me off." He brushed a flake of napkin ash off the satin lapel of his suit coat. "Or to punish me for a slight suffered."

"Well, you definitely seem distracted." She scoffed. "And I'll admit that I don't appreciate your arresting my son for that incident with his unfaithful girlfriend. But I'm not taking it out on your partner. If I wanted to leave an elven knife in someone, it'd be you yourself."

"I'd prefer it that way." He pulled his wallet from his back pocket and pulled out a hundred dollar bill. He passed it to her, but did not let go. "My threat still stands. Spread the word that my partners are off limits. If someone has a problem with me, they can meet me face to face."

He left her with the money and the threat and walked out of the shop. God help him, she was right. Intimidating people wasn't his style. He usually let his partners do that. He rubbed a gloved hand over his face and through his hair and leaned against the brick facade of the row of shops. *Vengeance is mine.*

Stay my hand, Lord. I'm not sure I can in my own strength.

"Word on the street is you finally ticked off the wrong people." A voice mocked from the doorway of the next shop.

"Chick's lawyers are in rare form today. I arrested you myself a couple hours ago." Dante stood and spun to face Wharton. "Those 'wrong people' wouldn't happen to be yours?"

"Not unless your pet had his throat ripped out." Wharton gave him a toothy grin. "When we send a message, we send it clearly."

"Well, I missed the memo on this one, unless the goal was just to make me mad." Dante clenched a fist. "If that's the case, it worked."

"You rely too much on humans, Dante. You police for them against your own kind, you favor their company over mythic company, and you make it clear you intend to keep it that way. And you wonder why someone offs your pet?" Wharton jabbed a finger into Dante's chest. "You're a traitor, but taking you out isn't an option, so someone picked this way instead. Can't say I blame them."

"I'm not a traitor. No being is above the law." Dante pushed his hand away and rubbed at the spot he touched with his handkerchief.

"*Human law.* Made and enforced without mythic input. You're their enforcer, the symbol of human oppression." Wharton growled. "It wasn't my people, but I don't fault the ones who did it. If it was me, I'd take out every partner you had until you got the point. Maybe once you see you can't count on those weaklings to have your back either, maybe you'll come around to where you belong."

"And maybe you'd unleash a demon you can't stop, Wharton." Dante lowered his voice and stepped closer to the werewolf alpha, his hands clenched tightly to fight the temptation to turn the bully into a pile of ash. "I may be bound by human laws, but I am still a mythic being, and immortal. Do not push me to the point that I decide justice would be better served without human aid, because you may find that means I serve it without human restrictions either."

He pulled his glove free as he turned, and set a trash can burning as he passed. Wharton's words scared him and made him furious. Was he right? Was this punishment for being a LEO for the humans? The mythics didn't really have a police force. Most guilds just dealt with issues in house, and for the most part PNI ignored any that didn't affect human kind. Or was Wharton just being spiteful because he hadn't had the guts to face Dante himself? Either way, someone tried to hurt

Rick to get to him, and that would never be okay. When Dante found out who it was, he'd leave a message that no member of the mythic community would fail to understand: Dante Brand's partner was off limits.

Chapter Thirteen

Dante's favorite place to go in DC was the Kennedy Center. He had a subscription to the National Symphony Orchestra, and enjoyed dressing up to hear both familiar classics and new modern concerts. Music seemed to be one of the only things that was truly timeless. A visit to the Symphony made him feel the curse of immortality less than anything else.

Except for tonight. Tonight instead of a tux and a concert, he was standing in the JFK Gallery reliving his worst failure. He stared at a portrait of the young president, one of the few who had seemed to see him as a person rather than an oddity, a weapon, or a slave. Perhaps it was because of their shared Catholic faith, one that had brought both of them unpopularity and persecution. Perhaps it was because they were both dismissed because of their youthful appearance. Perhaps it was simply a shared passion for the fine things in life. Whatever it was, Dante had taken the President's assassination personally. If Ruby hadn't taken out Oswald before Dante arrived in Dallas, he might have done it himself.

Failing to protect Rick felt very much the same. Though he hadn't known his new partner for long, he had already come to like him. He took all his partners' safety very seriously, and the thought that another one had been wounded because of him made him feel very, very reckless. Reckless enough to march straight to Vikas and demand the mythic guilds cooperate in hunting Rick's attacker.

Rick's out of surgery. Where ru? A text from Charles caught Dante halfway to the door. It was followed quickly with, Don't go making trouble. I don't want to be fishing you from the Potomac, or bailing you out of jail.

Considering that Dante's plan was to burn down the guild house if they didn't give him the assassins, he glared at the phone. The mythics wouldn't turn him over to the police, but the worst case scenario *did* end with Charles dragging the Potomac for him.

DON'T YOU DARE GO SILENT ON ME. I SWEAR, DANTE, IF YOU MAKE ME LOSE TWO AGENTS TODAY, I WILL MURDER YOU MYSELF.

Dante squeezed his eyes closed and took a deep breath as he made the sign of the cross. *Merciful God, grant that Rick's life be spared.* He dialed Charles' number immediately.

"Charles. What do the doctors say?" Emotion trembled in his voice. His boss's "lose two agents" comment frightened him almost as much as finding Rick lying in his own blood had.

"That you probably saved his life. That he has a chipped rib and a punctured lung. That he needed a blood transfusion." Charles sighed. "That he'll make a full recovery."

"Thank God." Dante felt his knees weaken and steadied himself with a hand against the side of the building.

"Do you have any idea who attacked him or why?" Charles asked.

"Not yet. The mythics seem to think it was to get to me."

"Wow. That wasn't obvious already."

"Elayna swears it wasn't the elves." Dante scoffed softly. She hadn't seemed terribly concerned about who it had been either.

"She claims they were framed? I guess I should have known she was smarter than to mess with you."

"Someone was not smarter than that, and I mean to find out who." Dante was standing outside the guild center now. "Vikas may know, or will be able to pressure the others to find out."

"I don't like the idea of you being out there without backup, Dante." Charles protested. "The people who tried to kill Rick, might try to kill you next."

"They attacked Rick precisely because they did not dare attack me, no?" Dante wasn't trying to be arrogant, it was just simply an obvious fact. One did not attack a harmless human if they could take out the mythic directly. "I will not provoke an attack, but I will not lie – I will not avoid a confrontation with the ones who did this either. Every mythic in the city must know that my partner is off limits or it will happen again."

"I'm not saying you're wrong, just..." Charles swore. "Don't forget there are limits to your immortality, *Chaud*. Vikas knows that. Please don't give him a reason to exploit it."

"Vikas and I may not see eye to eye, *Glace*, but he is a valuable ally. He is not a threat. The worst he would do is kill me once or twice to make a point."

"With friends like these..." Charles trailed off. "I'll keep you updated on Rick's condition, but I'd rather you were here when he woke up. Try to keep it quick."

Dante hung up and pocketed his phone, then knocked at the door. He preened carefully while he awaited an answer. Vikas was the closest thing to a leader the guilds had. The guilds respected Vikas, hopefully enough to help find Rick's attackers if he asked. Plus, he seemed to have grown attached to Pietro, his own human ally, and would understand the need for attacks on their human allies to not be left unpunished.

Arges opened the door. "Master Vikas has already retired for the night."

"I understand, and I would not visit at this hour if it was not an emergency." Dante wedged the toe of his Florsheims into the open door. "Someone stabbed my partner with an elvish blade earlier today, and I need Vikas's help."

Arges glared at him with his one eye, kicked Dante's foot out of the door, and closed the door in his face. Dante frowned and fingered the hem of his glove, trying to decide if he was desperate enough to burn down Vikas's door. Charles's warning cooled his fury and he nearly turned to return in the morning when the door swung open again.

"You got ten minutes." Arges opened the door to usher Dante in. He led him to the council chamber, a huge room with a massive antique table and high backed chairs, empty except for an auburn haired man with a narrow face and silk house robe sitting at the head of the table.

"Dante. Arges told me about your partner. You have my condolences." Vikas templed his fingers and frowned.

"I need more than condolences." Dante waved a gloved hand dismissively. "My partner will survive the attack, but I want the people responsible."

"Then you should be beating down Elayna's door, not mine."

"Elayna swears it was not one of hers." Dante placed his hands on the edge of the table and looked across it at Vikas. "I want the mythics to know my partner is off limits."

"Why would any mythic want to make you angry, Dante, seriously?" Vikas scoffed. "You're certain it wasn't an enemy of your partner? Someone who didn't realize who they were dealing with?"

Dante hesitated. He'd been sure, especially after his confrontation with Wharton. But what if it had been a personal vendetta against Rick? It would explain the utter foolishness of provoking him if the perpetrators didn't realize who Rick's new partner was. It didn't explain the elvish dagger, or how Rick had enemies in DC after only being there a few weeks.

"It is possible, but that explanation has its own problems and the Service is investigating the human angle." Dante shrugged. "I am concerned that someone of our kind has become cowardly enough to hurt our humans in our place. I am certain you can see the devastating consequences this would have if mystics began targeting humans."

"Hmmm." A troubled look crossed Vikas's face. "I still think you're understandably upset and overreacting, but I can't say I wouldn't feel the same if someone hurt Pietro. I will make some inquiries and reassert to the guilds that this won't be tolerated. Where can I find you if I hear anything?"

"Walter Reed Hospital." Dante took the hint and turned to go. He was used to people telling him he was overreacting, but this time Vikas was wrong. If anything, Dante was the very picture of restraint. Nothing was on fire yet, after all. "Regardless of who or why, I will not leave my partner unprotected again."

Rick lay in the hospital bed when Dante arrived. He was pale and still, with his eyes closed and a cannula delivering oxygen to him still. IV fluids and antibiotics trailed to a line in his left hand, which rested on top of the blankets beside him. Charles had said he'd awoken after the surgery, gave a statement, and asked for Dante. While Dante still wished he could be out investigating, both he and Charles had eventually agreed that he was more useful at Rick's side, making sure he was there when Rick awoke again, and that no one tried to finish what they started.

A pretty blonde sat in a chair beside the bed. Her clothes were fine, but mussed and her makeup was smeared from crying. Rick's girlfriend? Dante wasn't sure. Rick had mentioned leaving a girl in New York, but had said that long distance relationships were hard. Finding your boyfriend had nearly been killed changed priorities pretty quickly.

He cleared his throat as he entered the room. "Mademoiselle, I am Agent Dante Brand."

"Gracie George." She turned and looked at him and understanding dawned on her face. "Oh. You're Rick's new partner."

"I am, and I am deeply sorry for what happened." He took a deep breath and stepped closer to the bed, watching Rick's chest rise and fall reassuringly. "Has he awoken yet?"

"Not since I got here." She looked back at Rick and laid her hand on his free one. "What exactly *did* happen? I mean, he was stabbed, I get it, and Director Leon did say you saved his life, but that's all I know."

"Sadly, we ourselves know very little more than that either." Dante pulled a chair closer to the bed and sat beside her. "I went to go get dinner from a nearby food truck, and he returned to his hotel. He tried to call me, but did not answer when I took the call, so I went back to check on him. That was when I found him."

"Was it related to your case? Nevermind, you probably can't tell me that. Rick can never talk about his cases." She smoothed some hair from Rick's face as she continued without looking at Dante. "Did you know his dream is to protect the President? I always knew he'd end up in DC. I just wasn't ready for it to come now. I certainly didn't expect to meet him here this way. We'd planned for me to visit over Spring break. He would have an apartment by then and be able to show me the town. I sort of suspected he would propose on the Lawn. Seeing him like this–" Her voice cracked and trembled when she continued, "I don't know that I can do this for the rest of my life."

"Can you imagine *not* spending the rest of your life with him?" Dante sighed and placed a hand over the one she was using to hold Rick's. "I have sat beside my partner's hospital bed before. It *is* indescribably hard. But not having a partner to have my back as I investigate difficult cases would be impossible. I do my best to keep them safe, but I am only human, and humans fail. He is in the hands of God, as he will be if you take him as your husband, no? That is all one can ask for."

Gracie finally turned to look at him. "Wow, that was... Thank you. You're right of course." She gave him a narrow look. "You're really wise for a guy your age, no offense. I have a little brother your age, and my parents can barely keep him from livestreaming himself eating his lunch with his feet. I can't imagine him saying something like that."

Dante tried to hide a look of consternation. "I am quite older than I look."

A snort from the bed drew both their attention. Rick's laugh turned into a cough and he tried to press his hand to his side. Gracie buzzed for the nurse, while Dante tried to help his friend sit up. Rick finally took a long ragged breath. He looked at Dante with haunted memories behind his eyes. "Man, Dante, I thought I was done. Did you fly there?"

"No. I was barely in time. As I was telling Mademoiselle George, you were in the hands of God." Dante stepped back to allow the nurse to check Rick over.

"Gracie, good to see you." Rick gave her a weak grin." This is one of the finest hospitals in DC, I'm sure, but not exactly the first place I wanted to introduce you to when you came to visit."

"There will be plenty of time when you get better." She patted his hand while the nurse finished checking his vitals. "Director Leon is putting me up in the hotel you were in, at least until you get better, and Annette found a sub to take my class at least until the end of the week." She leaned forward and kissed his forehead. "By the time I leave, you'll be sick of me."

"That will never happen, though Dante may get sick of the both of us before that happens." Rick settled back as the nurse left the room.

"I spent a large portion of my life in France, I assure you the flirtations of a couple in love do not bother me." Dante forced a soft laugh. The attack on Rick and the lingering threat surrounding him had nearly destroyed a beautiful couple. And while he meant every word he'd said to Mms. George – he had absolutely no intention of abandoning his partner just because there was danger – he did find the desperation to avenge the attack return more strongly. It was not only he himself the attacker dared to mess with, but a good man and a gracious woman as well. "There are many things we will need to discuss once you are well, but for the time being, is there anything you can tell me about the attack?"

"Two ugly trolls attacked me with cosplay swords in the back of the hotel." Rick spoke slowly as if choosing his words carefully. "I tried to shoot them, but one got me under the arm. I woke up here."

"You are certain they were ugly and not as beautiful as women?" Dante asked seriously. Describing mythics to a non-believing human was always an interesting task, and they didn't need to frighten Mms. George further.

"Like a pair of goblins playing dress up. Does PNI have sketch artists, because I can do one if it helps." He yawned widely and grunted in pain.

"I will send one later today." Dante squeezed Rick's leg. "Now you must rest. Charles is anxious that I am working without a partner, and I am eager to clear this case as soon as possible." He squeezed tighter and lowered his voice. "This is unacceptable, Rick, and I mean to make it quite clear I will not tolerate it."

"Don't be an idiot. *I* will not tolerate it if you end up here or buried in a slab of concrete somewhere." Rick frowned. "You're not invincible, Dante, even if you all like to pretend you are."

Dante only hummed. He was very aware of his weaknesses, and thankful that most of his enemies were too intimidated by his reputation to think too hard about finding them, but his most obvious weakness lay in the hospital bed in front of him. Clearly whoever did this was either not brave enough or not smart enough to take him out directly. He needed to assert the futility of harming his partners as well.

"Rest well, my friend. With your girlfriend to care for you and me to protect you, you will be out of here in no time at all."

Chapter Fourteen

Rick hurt. A lot. He'd been released from the hospital with a list of care instructions and a new temporary home. Dante had suggested he move into his house at least until the guys who'd ordered the hit on him were found. Rick had been reluctant at first. It was, after all, a different thing to spend even your down time with your partner. But the first nightmare of the attack decided for him. He couldn't go back to the hotel he was at, and he was in no condition to find something else at the moment, so he'd have to take Dante up on his offer at least for a while.

"I think this is it?" Gracie said uncertainly as she pulled into the drive of a two-story brownstone. "Gosh, Rick, it looks old enough that George Washington could have lived here."

"It probably is." Rick started to laugh, but moved to get out of the car and the pain killed any desire for humor.

Dante pulled his door open and offered him his arm like a fancy manservant. Avoiding explaining Dante to Gracie was easy enough on the phone, in real life not so much. The man was so anachronistic, Rick was shocked she hadn't asked questions yet. So far she seemed to think he was just a cute quirky kid like her brother and all his friends. He took Dante's arm and leaned heavily on his partner as he got out of the car. Dante kept a worried eye on him, but didn't comment.

"I took the liberty of moving all your stuff from the hotel room to the room across from mine. It is a large, well furnished room and should serve your needs quite well." Dante's concerned look deepened as they slowed to mount the stairs to his porch. "It is however on the second floor, as they all are."

"It's fine. I won't be this weak for long, and I won't be a burden to you much longer than that." Rick gritted his teeth from the pain. Why did he leave the hospital again?

"You are not a burden. I am simply happy you are alive to care for. You may stay as long as it is beneficial to you."

"Wow, Dante, your house is like stepping into a museum!" Gracie called from the door. "I'm really impressed."

"What she really means is she's impressed you don't still live with your parents." Rick teased under his breath. He felt kinda bad for her brother Timmy, who would probably never hear the end of "Rick's young new partner who has his own house and actually says intelligent things, instead of living with his parents and filming unboxings of his Harry Potter socks."

Dante groaned. "Why can I not appear closer to your age when I resurrect? People do not question whether a thirty year old can function as an adult."

They joined her inside, and Rick kind of saw where her sense of awe came from. It was not a time capsule home from the American Revolution, but a collection of various eras as eclectic and anachronistic as its owner. The furniture seemed mainly Shaker, but a deep chair-and-a-half La-z-boy sat near the fireplace and a walnut mid-century modern buffet cabinet sat in the dining room. There was no television, but a state-of-the-art sound system and music collection dominated one wall. A massive impressionist painting of a phoenix in flight covered another. The kitchen looked like an old world relic, but the appliances seemed to be modern recreations rather than archaic museum pieces. It was also as immaculately clean and impeccably decorated as its owner was.

"I think I'm impressed also.This is way nicer than my apartment in New York." Rick walked to the music collection. It contained records, eight-tracks, cassette tapes, and CDs from every genre and across every era, but was heavily dominated by classical symphonies and operas.

Which kind of made sense, once you realized that symphonies and operas dominated music for most of the last five hundred years.

Dante shrugged. "I have a good job and few needs. The house is paid for and the furniture I have collected over time. Most of my money goes into clothes and music."

"I believe it." Rick carefully slid a copy of The Beatles Abbey Road from the collection. "Do you have any idea how much this stuff is worth?"

"Yes." Dante sounded very uncomfortable with the conversation, and Rick wasn't sure if it was because he didn't like talking about himself, or because Gracie was in the room. "Charles insisted that I get it appraised and insured when he was staying here."

"I didn't know the director stayed with you." Rick slipped the record back into place and changed the subject. "How long did that last?"

"I am sure you're quite tired. I can answer any questions you have later." Dante offered his arm again. "Can I show you to your room?"

So it was because Gracie was there. Rick took Dante's arm and leaned in closer, this time for privacy as much as support. "We could tell her. It might make life easier in the long run. I still hope to marry her eventually."

"In my experience, it rarely makes it easier in the long run," Dante said stiffly as they rounded the landing. "And if you truly wish to marry her eventually, you might be better off leaving it be."

They reached the second floor before Rick could ask him what he meant. And crossed to a large, well furnished room. It was decorated in a blue and silver color scheme, with dark blue walls above silver painted wainscoting, and silver threaded blue curtains covering the dormer window across from the door. It had a bedroom set that included a full bed, two bedside tables, two dressers and a high backed chair. A mirror was mounted to the wall over the tall dresser to the left and what looked to be a large silver engraving over the headboard to the right.

The adventure novel Rick had been reading at the hotel already sat on the bedside table next to a silver alarm clock.

"I took care to unpack your things so that you could use them as you recovered." Dante opened the closet to reveal Rick's clothes carefully hung. "You are of course welcome to reorganize them as you like. The decor may be changed to suit you better if you like, I only ask for the engraving to be relocated within the house if you do not wish it to stay here."

"No, no, it's fine." Rick looked at it more closely. It seemed to be some mythical scene he couldn't quite place.

Until Gracie squealed, "Oh, it looks like a fairy turning a peacock into a man. I don't know the story here, but the detailing is absolutely beautiful."

Rick saw it now. The fairy, the man rising from a fire, and three large birds near the man in the forest. He gave Dante a startled look.

"There is a legend in parts of Europe that there was once a very vain and beautiful phoenix who was bragging about his beauty to his fellows." Dante's voice grew soft and grave, and his accent even thicker. "The fairy, equally vain, demanded that the phoenix confess that she was more beautiful than he. The phoenix spread his wings and preened his brightly colored feathers. He foolishly told the fae that he had his beautiful feathers, but without her fine clothes she was nothing. Furious, the fae cursed him to an eternity as a featherless human. Satisfied that they were now on an equal standing, the fae repeated her demand, offering to give him back his natural form if he praised her beauty above his own. Humiliated, and furious, the phoenix refused. Legend says that he still walks the earth, and still refuses to give honor to the fae that cursed him."

"Aww, so phoenixes are basically mythological peacocks." Gracie reached up and touched the frame of the engraving.

"Basically." Dante laughed.

"But why didn't the phoenix just give in. It's not like he hasn't had enough time to get over his pride." Rick winced. That came out harsher than he had planned. It was *Dante's* pride they were discussing, not just some mythological character's.

"At first it was just pride, as the phoenix believed he could replace his lost feathers with fine clothes. Then it became a matter of principle, as the phoenix came to resent the fae's manipulation." Dante met Rick's eye with a fierce look. "Then it became a matter of purpose, as the phoenix found a life of his own as a human."

"It's a lovely house, Dante, thank you so much for taking care of Rick for me." Grace kissed Rick on the cheek. "I'm going to leave you to rest. I'll check in on you before I head home tomorrow."

"Thank you for coming, Gracie." Rick took both her hands in his and kissed her quickly on the lips. While he wished she didn't have to leave, he was getting very tired. "I'll look forward to tomorrow."

She blushed and left the room, laying a hand on Dante's arm as she passed.

Dante started to follow her out. "I will leave you to rest also. You are welcome to use the kitchen if you wish once you are well, but I will bring you dinner in the meantime." Dante looked past Rick at the engraving. "I may be expecting company tonight, so do not be alarmed if you hear voices."

Rick's eyes widened. "The fae? In the story? She's coming here?"

"She visits at least once a year to repeat her offer." Dante frowned at the picture as if remembering the events depicted in the engraving. "She will not harm you, but may make a general nuisance of herself, especially when I reject her again. That is why I risked telling the story. It is only fair you be warned."

"Why do you keep rejecting her? Five hundred years, and all you had to do to break the curse was tell her she's prettier than you?" Rick gave his proud partner an appraising look. "Surely even you aren't that vain."

"I nearly did a couple times." Dante shrugged. "But after the phoenixes went extinct and I found my place as an investigator for the humans, that temptation became less and less." He flashed Rick a reckless grin. "Besides, she really is not that beautiful. To lie to her would violate my dignity and my pride, no?"

A cold wind filled the room and Dante's smile froze and his eyes hardened defiantly. He lifted his head proudly and clenched a gloved fist beside him. Rick eased himself down onto the bed.

A beautiful woman with a spiteful face and glittering wings floated into the room.

"You know I can hear you, Dante Darling." She glared at him maliciously. "There's no reason to be nasty."

"Ravinia, I have better things to do with my night than to wait for you." Dante sniffed and folded his arms over his chest. "Let us get on with this so that Agent McCoy can get some rest."

"Your new partner? So soon? And you broke this one already as well?" The fae Dante had called Ravinia crossed the room to where Rick sat, cupped Rick's chin in her hand, and clicked her tongue. "I don't understand why you do this to yourself, Dante. This one is not more durable than the last. Why don't you ever pick a werewolf or vampire for a partner? Or even a fae?"

"You made me human, I have cast my lot in with them." Dante moved between her and Rick. "Your business is with me, he is my guest and of no concern to you."

"Oh, Dante, he can be very helpful." She floated close to Dante and purred in his ear. "Maybe he can help settle our centuries old dispute once and for all."

Alarm settled on Dante's face, and he grabbed the fae by the arm. "Ravinia, I protest. Do not involve him in this–"

With a flick of her hand, Ravinia threw Dante back against the dresser. "You will keep your hands to yourself, foolish bird."

"Dante?" Rick called worriedly. As weird as this was, he was getting a little immune to weirdness by this point. He was just glad Dante had waited until Gracie had left before he chose to insult a centuries old fairy.

Dante pushed himself to his feet carefully and wiped a trickle of blood from his mouth with his handkerchief. "I am fine, Rick. She causes trouble, but no real harm."

"But it's so much fun to cause trouble." She laughed meanly. "Rick, is it? Rick McCoy? Your partner is a stubborn and prideful fool. You look like a smart man. You think I'm more beautiful than he is, don't you?"

Rick laughed out loud. "Well, he's a guy, so, yeah." Dante gave him a withering look, which just made him laugh harder. He stopped with a gasp of pain and clutched his arm to his side.

"You *are* a smart man." Ravinia chuckled. She laid a hand on Rick's chest. "Now say it. Tell me I'm the most beautiful being in the world."

"Um... That's a pretty big leap from 'prettier than Dante.'" Rick's mind scrambled desperately for an answer that wouldn't get him in trouble. Gracie was far prettier than this vain, vindictive witch, and saying otherwise seemed like being disloyal to Gracie. On the other hand, he didn't really want to end up cursed eternally like Dante either. He gave his partner a panicked look.

"Ravinia, leave my partner alone, or I will turn you to ash right here." Dante's glove was off and the ball of fire cupped in his hand was already hot enough to warm the room. It also flickered in his golden eyes and gave an eerie glow to his rage-contorted face. His voice was still soft, but as cold and dark as death itself.

Fear lit Ravinia's eyes and she jerked her hand off Rick's chest as if he himself had turned to flame. She turned to Dante with a pout and a note of whine in her voice. "You're never any fun."

"Leave us, you vindictive witch." Dante snapped his fingers and the fire died. He pulled the glove back on as he continued, "I have no desire to return to my original form and will not concede to your manipulation. Nor will I let you manipulate my partner. Torment someone else."

"Bah. You'll change your mind. I'll be here waiting." She waved her hand and laughed as Dante's neatly styled hair turned a bright shade of blue. "In the meantime, just so you remember I won't be trifled with." With another mocking laugh, she disappeared.

Dante, frozen in rigid defiance when she waved her hand, seemed to melt in horror as soon as she was gone. "Please, by the love of all that's holy, tell me what she did *this* time?"

"She turned your hair blue." Rick, still not recovered from the look of murder on Dante's face only moments earlier, feared his partner's reaction to having his appearance messed with, so added quickly, "But hair is easy to dye, and colored hair is in right now anyway."

"Just my hair, praise the Lord. I can dye it, or it will return to normal the next time I resurrect." Dante relaxed and gave Rick a weary smile. "Last year she turned me into a circus clown. The clothes I could change, but the makeup and hair would not come out until I resurrected. I went out back and had Charles shoot me then."

"I'm not doing that, so you're stuck with the blue hair."

"No, *absolutely* not." Dante rushed to the bathroom in the hall to look in the mirror. "I'll be making an emergency appointment with my hairdresser the moment they open."

Chapter Fifteen

Three weeks of inactivity, of watching Dante leave every morning for work, of getting updates on their cases over dinner but not participating in them was driving Rick nuts. He could return to the office after four weeks, but would be off active duty for at least three more. At least after three weeks, he had the energy to get out of bed, get dressed, and move to the living room to watch movies on his phone, rather than staying in bed all day. He was quickly going stir crazy.

I really need to get Dante a TV.

He was on his fifth episode of CHiPs when Dante's call interrupted.

"I hate to do this to you, but I really need my partner." Dante's voice was low, as if trying not to be overheard. "You wouldn't possibly be feeling well enough to stand around a crime scene?"

Rick sat up straighter. Dante had barely let him move without supervision since he'd gotten out of the hospital. If he was calling for help, it had to be serious. "How bad?"

"I think I may be about to be arrested."

"What did you do?" Fear spiked down Rick's spine. Dante had repeatedly stated he would make sure no one messed with his partners again. Surely he hadn't done something too severe.

"Threatened the wrong people. There was another murder last night, and given the circumstances, they can't fail to suspect me. Please come as soon as you can. You're my alibi." Dante hung up without waiting for a response. A text with his location followed immediately.

Rick pulled on a jacket to hide the fact that he was wearing a sweatshirt, and drove to the address immediately. The place was cordoned off like every one of their crime scenes, and officers and gawkers buzzed around the perimeter.

WHERE ARE YOU? He texted before he even climbed out of the car. He was already tired and achy. He was definitely going to regret this later.

I'M ON MY WAY OUT.

The address in question was a fancy bakery with pink and white striped awnings over the plate glass windows and a giant illuminated cupcake for a sign that said "Takes the Cake Bakery" in flourishing script. Dante did indeed come out the door, a secret service agent in front and behind him, his head held high, and his face pale and grim. His face lit up when he saw Rick.

"Ah, my friend. Elayna was understandably unreasonable. I felt it best to surrender myself to the agents rather than to provoke her further."

Rick nodded to the familiar agents and fell into place beside Dante, trying not to breathe too heavily as he tried to keep up with the briskly walking trio. It was a testament to how much they trusted Dante that they allowed him to surrender without cuffs. Though Rick supposed cuffs would be pretty useless to a guy who could melt them with a touch. "You'll have to start from the beginning. I don't even know who Elayna is."

"Queen of the elves and the owner of that bakery there."

"Elves. Got it." Rick's aching side and shortness of breath were making it difficult for him to concentrate. He did remember Dante's suggestion on the phone that he had threatened the wrong people. "Why would you threaten the elves?"

Dante raised an eyebrow and nodded over to Rick's wounded side.

"Oh. Ah." Rick frowned. So this *was* about him.

"Elayna came in this morning to find the young lady who assists her had been murdered." Dante lowered his voice and anger flickered in his golden eyes. "It is quite horrible, Rick. Burns such as I would make. I do not fault them for suspecting me."

They'd reached the squad car and the agents were motioning for Dante to get in the back. Rick placed his right hand on the car leaned heavily against it to catch his breath.

"How can I help?"

"You can tell them that I no longer had a motive once I heard your testimony that your attackers were definitely not elves. You can tell them what time I was at the house this morning." Dante ducked into the car and looked up at him. "The murder happened between five and six this morning."

Rick snorted. Dante was up and primping that whole time. Rick had been restless and still unused to the noises of a roommate and had looked at the clock several times. "I can do that."

"You can come with me to face the Mythic Council, as I will have to answer to them as well. As queen of the elves, Elayna is a member and loudly demanded a tribunal." Dante looked at Rick's side again worriedly. "I am sorry. You should still be home resting."

"Yeah, I'm sure Ponch and Jon are going to miss me." Rick rubbed his side. As long as he took it easy, he should be fine.

Dante appeared confused.

"It's just a TV show, Dante. I've been sitting around for three weeks. A few hours out with you won't kill me."

"Hmm." Dante was clearly skeptical.

"You have no choice. See you at the office." Rick closed the car door and stepped back for it to pull out. There was no way he was leaving his partner out to dry because of what amounted to a really bad cut.

After a couple hours of interviews and an official recorded statement, Dante was free to go, but was relieved of his duties pending the Mythic Tribunal. Charles was sympathetic, but clear: innocent or not, his ability to work as the investigative liaison between mythics and humans was severely compromised as long as the mythics believed he was guilty.

"So we're on to the tribunal?" Rick asked through gritted teeth, trying to sound like it was no big deal.

Dante was clearly not fooled.

"We're off to get you in bed." His partner took him by his elbow and laid a guiding hand on his back. "The Mythic Council never meets before dusk, and you have been on your feet far longer than I am comfortable with already."

Rick didn't protest, or flinch at Dante's touch. He was too sore and tired to do either. Or to object when Dante held out his gloved hand to take the keys to Rick's Jeep.

He slept most of the drive home, then yielded without complaint to Dante tucking him into bed.

"Is there anything else I can get you?" Dante offered him a water bottle and a fistful of prescription medication.

"I'm fine, Dante, really." Rick took the pills and water and knocked them back quickly. "I just did too much. I can't just keep sitting around here."

Dante hummed softly. "Once you are cleared for physical activity, I will help you spar to get back to full strength. Until then, six weeks is just a blink in the grand scheme of time."

"Maybe to an immortal like you. To the rest of us, it feels like an eternity," Rick grumbled as he scooted down under the blankets.

"No, six weeks of inactivity feels like an eternity no matter who you are, especially when someone important to you is facing danger without you." Dante tucked the blankets around Rick's shoulders with a soft chuckle. "I broke my leg a year and a half ago and Wes persuaded me that shooting myself over a broken leg was a bit bombastic. I spent *three months* in a cast, and countless weeks of making every day leg day after that before I was functioning at full capacity. It did indeed feel like an eternity, but I got there, and you will too. If there is anything I can do to speed your recovery, I will do it gladly."

"Short of facing a mythic tribunal alone." Rick yawned.

"I am deeply sorry your baptism by fire continues even as you should be recovering. If there were any other way, I would take it." Dante flipped off the light switch. "We will discuss it later. I will wake you in time for you to shower, dress, and eat before we go."

"Yeah, just remember that *I* don't take two hours in the bathroom." Rick called after his partner as he closed the door.

"Yes, well, perhaps some of us take more pride in our appearance, no?"

Rick fell asleep with the vague discomfort of knowing he'd just been insulted by the vainest man he knew.

He woke to a knock at the door and the rich smell of homemade chicken soup.

"An old Florentine recipe, better than any drug modern medicine can prescribe." Dante set a tray with a steaming bowl of soup and a thick slice of buttered bread in Rick's lap.

"I've got a knife wound, not the flu." Still, the soup smelled better than the canned stuff he'd been making himself while Dante was at work. "Tell me, how is it you speak fluent Italian and know an old Florentine recipe if you're originally from France?"

"I did not say 'originally', only that I spent much of my life there, which is true." Dante sat halfway on the arched footboard and gestured to the engraving on the wall. "Since the day phoenixes were created to foreshadow *THE* Resurrection, my kind had lived for millennia in the woods outside Milan. After I was cursed, I wandered in the villages finding no place for myself, being neither phoenix nor truly man. A man you know as Leonardo de Vinci found me and recognized my talent for opposing the darker forces of nature. I served him and his patrons until his death in France where I continued as agent of the French Crown until the French Revolution drove me to your shores."

"Wait, did you meet George Washington?" Rick stopped shoveling soup and gestured at Dante with his spoon.

"I have served every one of your presidents." Dante shook his head. "Americans. You all think history started in 1776."

"The important stuff did." Rick snorted. He set the empty bowl aside. "I need a shower, and I'll be ready to go. You might want to put on something that looks less like an advertisement for an embroidery shop before we go. They might take you more seriously."

Dante gave him a withering look as he straightened the blazer made of deep red jacquard with gold flames embroidered on the satin lapels. "I'll have you know –"

"I don't care. And they won't either." Rick raised a hand to stop Dante's protest. "These are grave accusations, and you need to dress accordingly. Do you even own a basic black suit?"

Dante's offended look was all the answer he got.

"What do you wear to testify in court?" Rick sighed. Probably nothing in Dante's whole closet could be classified as "basic." "Surely in half a millennium of service you've had to do that."

"I have a suit for that, yes." Sobriety reached Dante's eyes. "If you think it's necessary."

"You're on trial here, Dante, whether you like it or not. And dressing like a blasted macaroni isn't going to win you any points."

"Ah, when good suits were easier to find."

"Just get changed." Rick rolled his eyes and pointed to the door.

Chapter Sixteen

Rick had time to shower, put on his own black suit, and watch half an episode of CHiPs by the time Dante changed into a tailored black cashmere suit with black satin lapels embroidered all over with black thread. Rick sighed and shook his head. He supposed that was probably the best he was going to get out of the fashion conscious phoenix. Besides, no suit was going to make up for the red spiked quiff that made Dante look like his head was on fire, or the youthful face that never quite looked serious.

Except now. Dante's expression was quite sober as he climbed into the car. He sat for a moment and fingered his rosary silently, before finally starting the car.

"That bad?" Rick started to feel a little nervous about this meeting himself. His testimony had been basically a formality to free Dante. With an alibi and no motive, the human courts of law had nothing to hold him on. Rick supposed he had assumed the Mythic Tribunal would be as easy to deal with. Dante's attitude now said otherwise.

"Politics play as large a part in this hearing as facts, and Elayna is a powerful member of the Council." Dante shrugged as he pulled his Firebird out onto the street. "I *have* allies in the Council, more than I do enemies, but the enemies are... more assertive than the allies at times."

"In other words, instead of an impartial jury of your peers, you're being judged by a group of powerful people you may have recently ticked off." Yeah, that sounded just. "Isn't this why PNI exists? To manage Mythic crimes?"

"Crimes that involve both mythics and humans, yes. Elayna has charged me with murdering her assistant and seeks vengeance for the offense. She does not want human justice, she wants blood." Dante flashed him a rueful grin. "Much as I did after you were attacked."

"You probably should have worn a cheaper suit then." Rick grunted. It was becoming less clear to him why his partner insisted on spending thousands on suits that he was just going to burn up anyway.

"Ah, *mon ami*. Elayna and the council would make sure I would not need the replacement." Dante gave a soft, melancholic laugh, as if something Rick had said was amusingly sad.

"Wait," Rick sat up straighter in horror. "Are you saying they'd end you *permanently*?"

"They have done it to other immortals before when they felt the crime particularly warranted it, though simple murder is not usually enough." Dante parked the car in front of an ancient stone building not far from his own home. It looked like it had originally been a nice home, a little newer than the colonial era pictures Rick had seen, but not by much. Dante gave him a bright smile that nearly hid the fear lingering in his golden eyes. "But that is why you are here, no? So you can help ensure I avoid that fate."

"I will do anything in my power to help you." Rick already hadn't liked the thought that even his testimony might be unable to save Dante's mortal life, but the thought that all his partner's immortal lives lay in the hands of a panel of fantasy creatures with an entirely arbitrary sense of justice just made him angry. *Dear Jesus, please bless our efforts here. Let us get them to see reason.* A mental image of himself punching a matronly elf in the face rose up in his mind and he shook it off. That was definitely not going to help either of them. *And help me not to do or say something to make it worse.*

"May the Savior show His favor to us today." Dante made the sign of the cross, took a deep breath, checked his reflection in a polished silver urn in the marble floored foyer, and adjusted his jacket collar. He led Rick to a pair of carved double doors in the back. A large man in an ill fitting suit and only one eye stood guard in front of the doors.

"A cyclops? For real?" Rick leaned close and whispered.

"After all the things you've seen with me, a man with one eye is hard to believe?" Dante laughed softly. He nodded to the cyclops and reached for the worn brass door handle. "Arges. I believe the Council is expecting me."

"Dante. Your human stays out here." Arges the Cyclops stepped between Rick and Dante to block Rick from the entrance. "You know humans aren't allowed inside the Council chamber."

"Unless the Mythic Council has rejected any pretense of seeking justice, they will allow Agent McCoy to enter to testify on my behalf." Dante's soft voice held none of the trepidation he'd shown in the car and his eyes met Arges's single one boldly.

Arges looked from Dante, to Rick, to the door, then sighed loudly. "I'll ask Vikas. Don't go anywhere."

"Vikas?" Rick whispered once the cyclops bouncer disappeared inside the room.

"He's a kitsune – fox shifter – and the current president of the Council. He's an ally, but will take a neutral position in this hearing, as befitting his position."

"Kitsune. Of course." Rick shook his head. "You know my little sister watched cartoons more believable than this. Like the one with the talking ponies."

"Kelpies? They're represented by the queen of the merfolk."

"No, not kelpies. I don't even know what a kelpie is. Remind me to Google that when we're done here." Rick rolled his eyes as the door opened again to the sound of internal arguing and a harried looking cyclops.

"Vikas says your human may testify as long as he is silent unless addressed and respects the sovereignty of the Council." Arges looked at Rick as if waiting for agreement.

"I agree to keep my mouth shut and respect the Council." Rick figured being silent would cover for the disrespectful words he was already certain he'd be tempted to say. Like, *Sovereignty? The only sovereignty in this city resides on Pennsylvania Avenue.* It was in everyone's best interest if he kept silent.

Arges made a confused face at Rick's intentional rewording of his instructions, but didn't push it. Instead, he just opened the door and announced their presence, "Dante Brand, phoenix, here to face charges laid to his account by the Council, and Rick McCoy, human."

The room was huge – by Rick's estimation, it occupied the vast majority of the ground floor – but it was still nearly filled by a massive, polished wood table lined on both sides with high-backed chairs. In each chair sat a sober-faced man or woman, presumably something other than human, though most passed as human at first glance. Rick recognized the werewolf he'd punched in the nose and the vampire makeup saleswoman among the Council members, and assumed the stately blond with a grief flushed face sitting to the right of the head of the table was Elayna the elf queen. At the head sat a thin man with an angular face, reddish brown hair, and long sideburns. He wore a black polo shirt and a pair of jeans carefully tailored to allow his five tails freedom of movement. A trench coat hung on the corner of his chair.

"Before we begin, Dante, the Mythic Council would like to state for the record that your insinuation that the Council is anything less than just offends the Council deeply." Vikas rested his elbows on the table and templed his fingers. "And you, human, be aware that you are here only as a gesture of our gracious indulgence."

"Gracious indulgence" didn't sound too much to Rick like "commitment to a fair trial" but he inclined his head anyway and said, "The Council's graciousness is appreciated."

"Let the charges against Dante Brand be read before the Council." Vikas nodded to a short Irishman next to him.

The little man stood up on the chair and cleared his throat. "Dante Brand, phoenix lately cursed to be a man, is charged with the wanton, savage murder of Annika Moore by fire, and for disloyalty to the Mythic race."

Rick risked a sideways glance at his partner. Even if his testimony cleared him of the first charge, his presence might be enough to convict him of the second. Dante stood ramrod straight with a defiant look and one hand clenched tightly at his side while the other was plunged deep into the pocket holding his rosary. His expression didn't change at the reading of the charges, as if he'd expected them.

"The members of the Council have been provided with the details of the murder, and have made themselves quite familiar with the unique method of the crime." Vikas frowned at Dante. "What do you say for yourself, Brand?"

"I had neither opportunity nor motive to murder Ms. Moore, as my partner can testify." Dante's voice was as quiet and calm as always as he gestured to a tall, muscular man sitting on the left side of the table. "And both you and Naar the dragon king are proof that I am not the only mythic being with the power to kill in this manner."

"You were literally the only mythic being in my bakery burning stuff last month." The elderly elf woman stood from her chair and screamed at him. "And this human shouldn't even be here. His testimony is worthless. Everyone knows that humans will lie for their mythic allies. The only reason Dante is free and not in some human prison is because both his partner and the director of PNI are loyal to him."

Rick ground his teeth to keep from speaking out of turn. He'd never once lied in a deposition or trial, and he certainly wasn't about to start, even for his partner.

"Elayna herself can testify that she settled my dispute with the elves before I left the bakery that night." Steel threaded Dante's voice as he looked at Vikas. "And the Council agreed to hear Agent McCoy's testimony. We all seek justice for Ms. Moore, but you will not find it by convicting me."

"Agent McCoy." Vikas nodded to him. "You came here to speak for your partner. The Council will take your testimony into the proper account when you have finished."

Proper account. Yeah, Dante is toast. Rick briefly wondered how long they could survive an escape attempt from this kangaroo court before he spoke up with the same measured calmness Dante displayed. "I'd already told Dante my attackers weren't elves. PNI's investigation moved in an entirely different direction the moment I woke up in the hospital. So unless your breed of elves are short, ugly trolls, he had no motivation to hurt Ms. Moore. Besides, he was in the bathroom making himself look pretty from at least five to seven that morning. He answered my knock a half dozen times, and he stuck his head out to shoo me back to bed three times – just so you don't get any ideas about him turning on the shower and sneaking out the window. He couldn't have killed Annika Moore."

"Thank you, Agent McCoy, that will be all." Vikas cut him off with a wave. "You will remain here and silent as a material witness to the second charge."

"Most mythics take human allies, Vikas, and most of the mythic guilds are as closely allied to their human counterparts as I am to PNI. Many even marry humans." Dante scanned the members of the Council, eliciting a variety of reactions from shame to defiance as he met their eyes. "There is no disloyalty in any of that."

"*You're* the only one that has allied with humans against the mythics." Wharton growled.

"No, I help keep the peace between mythics and humans by making sure crimes that might draw unwanted attention to the existence and activities of the mythic races are solved tactfully so that human mythic relations can continue as they always have." Dante gave him a scolding look. "Seeking peace between factions is not inherently disloyal to one."

"Except that you have failed at that miserably as well." Laysha the vampire queen turned her phone so that they could see Lynch's video. "You're responsible for this, Dante. You should have dealt with this stupid human years ago."

Uncertainty flickered in Dante's eyes as he glanced at the video. "Human laws –"

"That's precisely the problem!" Wharton slammed his fist on the table and stood. "If we must have a liaison between mythics and human law enforcement officers, we need one that puts mythic interests first."

A murmur threaded through the Council and heads began nodding thoughtfully. Rick bit his lip. This wasn't going well.

"Not all mythic interests are werewolf interests." A small man with reddish hair stood on his chair and glared at Wharton. "Dante also represents the less aggressive guilds where *your kind* would trample our rights."

"Representing leprechauns is *your* job, Finnegan, as *king* of the leprechauns." Wharton smashed his fist into the table. "For that matter, the president of the humans should treat directly with us, instead of through *him*."

"Exactly. Why do we need a liaison at all? We should rise up and demand our place as equals to the humans," Laysha shouted. "If Dante wants to be an enforcer, let him enforce for us. We can make the humans fear mythics again."

About half the mythics hollered their agreement – the more aggressive looking races, Rick noticed – and half of the remaining members continued to murmur in worried tones.

"My purpose is to enforce the laws of God where humans are too weak to do so." Dante raised his voice only enough to be heard over the tumult. Rick was frankly shocked the other agent hadn't lost his cool yet. It was all *he* could do to keep from breaking his promise to keep quiet himself. "The only people who should fear me are murderers."

"Like you murdered Annika?" The elf woman snapped.

"I did not murder anyone. We're past that."

"You're responsible for 'enforcement.' Four humans have been attacked or killed in the last month – including your own – and PNI has yet to make a single arrest." The elf queen pointed at him with a bony finger. "Even if you didn't *kill* her, if you had done your job, she'd still be alive."

"Enough!" Vikas stood. "The Council has heard enough to deliberate. Dante, take your human back into the foyer and await our decision."

Chapter Seventeen

Dante nodded grimly and gestured for Rick to follow. They didn't speak until they were sitting back outside the chamber.

"Thank you for your support, my friend." Dante dug into his pocket and handed Rick his car keys. "I want you to go. If their decision goes as I fear, I do not want you caught in the middle."

"I'm not leaving." Rick pushed Dante's gloved hand back at him. "What kind of partner would I be if I bailed on you the moment things looked bad?"

"I appreciate your loyalty, but..." Dante leaned closer to Rick so that Arges couldn't overhear. "For nearly a century, Vikas has led with the best interests of the mythic community in mind. And for nearly a century, I have been able to persuade him that PNI is part of that." He tucked the keys into Rick's hand and closed Rick's fingers around them. "If my failure, and Lynch's video have convinced him otherwise, I fear what the less peaceable factions may persuade him to do. He feels no duty to humans, and certainly none to you. Besides, someone needs to warn Charles, no?"

"I'll send him a text." Rick pocketed the keys and pulled out his phone. "Wharton has already tried to kill you permanently once and that vampire chick –"

"Would just as soon see both of us dead. Charles cannot *save* us, PNI has no jurisdiction inside this building. He can only be warned that unrest is coming." Dante's voice took a hard tone and his grim expression made his face appear older. "I outrank you, Agent McCoy, and order you to leave immediately. I will handle the Council alone, and face their judgment alone."

"If PNI has no jurisdiction here, then you don't outrank me here either." Rick looked up from his text as he hit send. "So, I refuse."

"Humans are only welcome in this building by invitation. If I say the word, Arges will escort you out." Dante raised an arm to signal for the bouncer at the door.

"You wouldn't." Rick grabbed his arm and pulled it down, grimacing a little at the sharp movement.

"If it saves your life, yes." Dante jerked his arm free.

"You signal for that one-eyed brute and I will punch you in the face so hard, Arges will be wondering if he should clear the building for a resurrection." Rick hissed. "You're not cutting me out. The only way I'm leaving is if you're with me. Partners have each others' backs. If our roles were reversed, Satan himself couldn't drag you from that room, a few of his minions aren't going to scare me off."

Dante sat back and glared at him for a moment, as if trying to decide whether to push the argument further. Rick rather hoped he wouldn't, since getting in a knock down fight with the phoenix in the mythic guild house wouldn't really help their cause right now. Finally his partner shook his head.

"I pray you live to regret this decision." Dante pulled the rosary from his pocket and put it over his head.

"If we *both* live, I won't regret it at all." *Lord, please help us both to walk away.*

Dante chuckled. "I suppose not." The door opened and one of the inside cyclops bouncers stuck his head out and spoke to Arges. Dante crossed himself as he stood. "Either way, our time is up."

The cyclops bouncers escorted them to their places standing at the foot of the table, and stood guard closer than before as Arges closed the door behind them. Rick scanned the faces of the Council members. The leprechaun and something else that seemed to favor Dante stared down at their hands. Wharton and Laysha and a couple of the more vicious looking members looked at Dante triumphantly. Vikas looked grim. Rick drew himself up taller. That the wrong side won was clear. Whether there was any way he could keep his partner from being killed wasn't so much. *Show me the way to help him.*

"Dante Brand, fae cursed phoenix, step forward to receive your judgment," Vikas intoned solemnly. He continued after Dante silently complied, "This Council finds you guilty of Annika Moore's murder by negligence and of choosing humans over your own kind."

"Thanks to my curse, humans are equally my kind," Dante replied softly. "Perhaps more so because there are no other phoenixes left for me to prefer."

"Then your sentence is from your own mouth." Vikas glared. "Either you will resign from PNI, swear allegiance to the Council, and take your place as an enforcer for the Council; or this Council will summon the fae that cursed you and demand she release your curse and return you to your natural form."

Dante laughed aloud. "She will no more submit to you than I will. The terms of my curse require me to admit her to be the most beautiful, and I will not. She will not release me from the curse any other way."

"Then resign from PNI and take your place here." Vikas's face was getting red and his voice was frustrated.

Dante was silent for a long moment, his hand still in the pocket with the rosary, and Rick held his breath. Dante had said that he had found his purpose as a human and had no desire to return to his natural form. But helping the humans was his purpose, so Rick couldn't see him resigning from PNI either.

"I will not." Dante finally answered, his face pale and his voice firm. "I have done nothing wrong, and will not consent to be the slave of those who would use me as a soldier rather than a peacekeeper."

"I RECOMMEND YOU RETHINK that, Dante. The Council will not allow you to continue in opposition to the interests of the mythic community." Vikas tapped the table with his finger. "One last time. Do you choose to return to your natural form or to work as an enforcer for the Council?"

Dante finished a Hail Mary. Returning to life as a phoenix was worse than death, and placing himself under the authority of council members like Wharton and Laysha defied his purpose in living. He had no choice. He could only pray they took it out on him alone. He gave Rick an apologetic look, pressed the crucifix at the end of his rosary to his lips and took a deep breath. "With God as my witness, I will not yield."

"Then may your God have mercy on your soul." Vikas gestured to the cyclops bouncers that had escorted Rick and Dante in.

The pair of cyclops pulled Dante's arms out to his sides before he could react and leaned against his back between his shoulder blades to force him to his knees. Their grip kept him from reaching his gloves, and the awkward posture disrupted his balance enough to keep him from retaliating. Rick made an indignant noise beside him, so he twisted his neck as much as he could to flash his partner a warning glare. The less attention Rick drew to himself the better chance he had for survival.

"Your refusal to submit to your sentence has left the Council with no choice." Vikas's tails flicked behind him as he stood and rounded the table to stand before Dante. "You are condemned to death by beheading. To remove the risk of you resurrecting, your head and body will be buried separately from each other after the vampires have sufficiently desecrated them."

Dante's heart stuttered and a cold chill ran down his back. The time he'd been dumped in Lake Michigan, he'd resurrected the moment his resurrection fire could ignite. They meant to corrupt the virtue that allowed him immortality in the first place. Fear that whatever they did to prevent his resurrection to this world would prohibit his resurrection to the world to come spread the ice of terror through his veins. *Soul of Christ, sanctify me. Body of Christ, save me.*

Laysha crouched in front of Dante and lifted his chin so she could look into his eyes. "Representatives of your faith have often used sacred icons such as crosses and holy water to keep our kind from resurrecting. I have often wondered what it would take to return the favor to you."

"Suffer me not to be separated from thee. From the malignant enemy protect me," Dante picked up the middle of the ancient prayer out loud and she dropped his head in disgust.

"Perhaps replacing his heart with that of an innocent man." She circled around to Rick and drew a sharp fingernail across his chest.

"Vikas, no!" Dante grunted as he struggled in vain against the two cyclops. "Agent McCoy is not under your jurisdiction. Send him on his way in peace."

"He made his choice when he returned to the council chamber to await your judgment." Vikas turned his back on them and went back to his chair. "They're yours, Laysha. Do what you must, but don't do it here."

Two vampires flanked Rick, grinning at him stupidly. The icy terror threading Dante's veins turned quickly to the fire of burning rage. Not again. He'd lost Wes to vampires, and had nearly lost Rick in the attack a few weeks ago. He would not let them touch him. Vikas and the whole council could burn in his resurrection fire as the building crumbled at his feet before that happened. He pushed up with his feet and snapped his elbows up and back into the faces of the cyclops guards, blinding them both. One let go, but the other wrenched Dante's shoulder as he staggered back. Dante turned to keep from getting his arm pulled from its socket and put all his displaced weight into a jab to the cyclops's exposed throat. Now the cyclops let go with a howl, but Dante was too off balance to keep his feet. He fell to his hands and knees with his back to the council.

"Subdue him, but don't kill him here!" Vikas yelled as the room buzzed with cries of fear and anger.

"Hold the human!" Laysha screamed. "Surrender, Dante, or you lose another partner to my men."

"If my partner is harmed, I will burn this whole accursed guild house to the ground after I incinerate everyone in it." Wrath threatened to blind Dante as he pushed himself to his feet, stripped the gloves off his hands, and threw them to the marble floor. The two vampires held Rick on either side. One of them had him by the hair to bare his throat to the other. "Let. Him. Go."

The two stupid vampires looked from him to Laysha in fear, unsure of who to obey. Dante didn't wait for them to decide. He grabbed them both by their own throats and held them as they turned to ash in his hands. He turned his attention to Laysha

"Stop him!" Layash shrieked as she scrambled behind Vikas's chair and cowered there. "Vikas, do something!"

A cyclops guard grabbed Dante by his right arm. Dante spun and grabbed his face. The second got smart and fired a gun at Dante twice instead of coming in arm's reach. Dante formed a ball of fire between his hands that he used as a shield to melt the incoming bullets, then flung the ball at the cyclops, who screamed as it engulfed him.

"Yes, Vikas, call them off." Dante stepped to the heavy council table and leaned on it with both hands. Council members scrambled away as the fire swept down the table toward Vikas.

"How dare you!" Vikas stood, glowering through the flames at Dante.

"How dare *you*!" Dante pointed a bare finger at Vikas as he formed a ball of fire in the other, taking care to keep his partner in sight to ensure one of the council members scattering from the conflagration like cockroaches didn't get a foolish idea to touch Rick again. "You listened to evil council and corrupted justice to the extent that you were a consenting party to the attempted use of dark arts against an innocent man and to the foul experiment of corrupting another's soul. With God as my witness, I should use my fire to purify this council of any mythic who voted to approve this abominable act."

"This council does what it must!" Vikas slammed his fist into what remained of the still burning table. "If you cannot support that, may you be doubly cursed to be banished from the guilds. Embrace the humans. You've clearly chosen them anyway."

"Knock it off, both of you!" Rick stepped between them and raised a hand to Dante. "I know why Ms. Moore was killed."

ALEXANDRA GILCHRIST

Chapter Eighteen

"Wait!" Rick stepped between his partner and the angry guild leader. "I know why Ms. Moore was killed." *Four humans have been attacked or killed in the last month – including your own – and PNI has yet to make a single arrest.* Thank the Lord he did, sort of. Maybe it was enough to get them a break.

Everyone in the room froze and every eye turned to him, including Dante's, which still held the murderous fire that had driven him to turn the vampires to ash. Not that Rick hadn't appreciated getting those things off his back before they bit him, but he'd be seeing the look on Dante's face in his nightmares for a while.

"Ms. Zanotti, the sailor, myself, Ms. Moore – we all *did* have something in common: we were all humans connected to important mythic beings." Vikas gave him a look that said, Is that all, stupid human? Rick stumbled over his words as he continued hurriedly. "And at least two of the attacks we know were set up to frame another mythic race for the crime – the trolls that attacked me using an elvish blade and conveniently leaving it for Dante to find, and the people who murdered Ms. Moore leaving burn marks only someone like Dante could make while Dante was clearly otherwise occupied. It wouldn't surprise me if the others were frames as well. What if this –" Rick gestured to Dante and Vikas facing off over the smoldering table – "is why?"

Dante straightened from his battle posture and brushed the flames from his hands. "To incite civil war among the mythics?"

"Or to incite the mythics against the humans." Vikas rounded the table to their side.

"The endgame of killing me and my partner, I'd wager," Dante said softly as he took a protective position at Rick's side.

Vikas gave him a withering look, but did not deny it.

"Or to incite the humans against the mythics. Remember Lynch's video?" Rick tried not to flinch away from his partner's bare hands, but having watched him just burn three people and a table with a touch, he was a little less successful than he'd have liked. He paused to retrieve Dante's gloves from where he'd dropped them and slapped them against his partner's arm. Whatever the mechanism, they were apparently the only thing that kept him from burning literally everything and everyone around him. "Is there anyone that would benefit from a mythic war?"

Dante chuckled as he pulled the gloves on and brushed ash from his suit. "I'd like the answer to that as well, Vikas."

Vikas glowered at him as the Council members silently gathered around them, the battle lines from earlier even more clearly shown by who the members chose to stand behind.

"All mythic creatures benefit from overthrowing the human oppressors," Wharton snarled. "Even if you're so sold to them you'd rather see us continue in slavery."

"Hold on, no one's in slavery." Rick interposed again. The last thing they needed was to reignite the fighting again.

Dante laid a gloved hand on Rick's shoulder and pulled him back slightly with a frown. "If you want me to address mythic grievances with the president, I will do so willingly. I will not countenance wanton violence. The werewolf and vampire solution to everything will just make things worse."

"You'd better watch who you say things like that to, or phoenix-kind might just go extinct." Wharton stepped forward to get in Dante's face, but was blocked by Vikas's arm.

"Many, many people have tried, human and mythic alike – including you yourself. And yet, here I am." Dante swept Rick behind him with his arm, unbuttoned his own collar and pulled it away from his neck. "Bite me, Wharton, let's see how this ends and who remains."

"Not today, Wharton. We don't need any more fire in here." Vikas kept his arm up and glared at Dante. "He is right, many mythics believe we would be better off without the humans."

"And if the view count on Lynch's video is any indicator, a lot of humans think they'll be better off without mythics." Dante pointed out.

"And, didn't Lynch sort of imply he was jealous of humans who found mythic partners?" Rick suddenly realized this wasn't narrowing anything down at all.

"Lynch is your problem, Dante. Laysha is right. You should have dealt with him a long time ago." Vikas pointed out.

"If I find he's behind this in any way, I will deal with him accordingly." Dante nodded to Vikas, and lowered his voice. "And you would do better for the mythic community if you would refuse to listen to those who would lead you to corruption and violence. I will not quickly forget what you allowed today."

"And the Council will not quickly forget where your allegiance lies." Vikas returned. "You have a long way to go to prove worthy of the honor of being reinstated in the Council."

"And you have a long way to go to prove it is indeed an honor." Dante sniffed as he turned to go. "You can start by letting me know if you learn of any mythics with a clear vendetta against humans – apart from the obvious members of your own Council of course." Rick didn't miss that Dante made sure he was physically between Rick and the vampire queen as they left the council chamber, or the deadly look that passed between them. "I will handle things from the human side."

"You were not dismissed!" Vikas called after them.

"You made it quite clear you didn't want us here when you tried to kill us." Rick turned and waved, then followed Dante out the door.

They were silent until they were clear of the building and back in Dante's car. Rick passed him the keys to the vehicle and slumped down into the passenger's seat as the exhaustion and pain of his previous injuries demanded attention now that the adrenaline of nearly being killed was waning.

"Are you certain you are unharmed?" Dante asked tightly, glancing at him as he pulled the car onto the road. His tone made it clear he at least was still quite high on blood lust.

"Yep. Fine. I'm totally used to getting out of bed when I'm recovering from being stabbed to turn around and be held hostage by evil, blood crazed vampires who want to use my heart in a dark ritual." He dropped his head back against the seat and closed his eyes. An odd noise between a grunt and a squawk from his partner made him open one eye and look at him. "I'm fine, Dante, seriously. Nothing a pain killer and a long nap won't fix."

The car was silent again as Rick grappled with the memories of those tense few minutes when it looked like he and Dante's partnership was over. The look on Dante's face and the sheer killing power he'd displayed were balanced by the fact that the deadly agent had used those powers to save his life, and had made clear that those powers were dedicated to good.

More difficult to deal with was the memory of the vampire's hands at his throat, the hunger in their eyes, and their queen's words describing what they planned to do. He rubbed his neck unconsciously. *Thank you, Lord, that Dante is on my side.*

"Thanks for stopping those vampires back there." Rick wanted to scream, throw things, or punch his fist through Dante's windshield, but he just lay there feeling an odd combination of numb and crazy. "And remind me not to get on your bad side."

"Someone told me that partners have each other's backs." Dante chuckled. "And that admittedly was a more extreme reaction than usual due to the extreme nature of their threats." The humor faded from his face. "Facing death is an inconvenience for me. Facing an eternity of corruption, and knowing they planned the same fate for you – I could not countenance that."

"I'm not saying that whole thing wasn't terrifying – because it really was – but eternity is one thing I'm *not* scared of." Rick peeked at him again. "Not saying I want to punch the next ticket, just that I know where I'm going."

"Things are not quite as clear for me." Dante wiggled a hand uncertainly. "I am confident in my relationship with Christ, yes, but I have died more times than I can count. I was dead for thirty-eight hours before Charles was able to get me pulled out of Lake Michigan. None of those times were any different from sleeping. I have always assumed I would be alive to meet my Savior at His return. But their plan to desecrate my body to keep me from ever resurrecting again?"

He paused to collect his thoughts. Rick glanced over to see his partner's pale face and flushed cheeks and went back to pretending to sleep to give Dante privacy.

Dante caught his breath and ended huskily, "I am ashamed to admit I am less than confident of the effects of that."

"'Fear not them which kill the body, but are not able to kill the soul,'" Rick quoted without opening his eyes. "The only one who has power over your soul is Christ, no matter what disgusting thing they planned to do to your body. You've lived through enough nasty periods of history to know that if humans could figure out how to damn each other, they'd have done it by now. They haven't, because they can't. No creepy vampire has power over the blood of Christ."

Dante was silent for a long moment. He finally blew out a slow breath. "Thank you, *mon ami*. You are right of course. I was wrong to worry."

Rick scoffed. "I'm pretty sure they don't offer Theology of Mythology at Bible college, and I'm a detective, not a theologian. I think we can both be forgiven for a bit of confusion.

"Speaking of confusion." Rick sat up and looked around as they parked in Dante's driveway. "Shouldn't we be heading to the office to make a statement and warn Director Leon the mythics are threatening to rise?"

"Charles is on his way here. I texted him and told him that you were hurt and needed to go to bed. He can take our statements here." Dante stepped out of the car and went to unlock the front door without waiting to listen to Rick's objection.

Not that Rick had one. He really did need a pain killer or four and a three-day nap. He sighed and dragged himself out of the car and up the stairs to the house. Dante watched him critically as he held the door, but thankfully did not comment on how slow moving he was.

There was no way Rick was going to bed knowing the director was on his way over, so he settled for a long, hot shower and a change of clothes to get rid of the vampire ash. By the time he came back downstairs, delicious smells came from the kitchen.

"What do you know, he cooks, too." Rick teased as he leaned against the arched entry to the kitchen. "Wait 'til I tell Gracie. She might just suggest her brother come live with you for a while to learn some real skills."

"It may surprise you to know that DC didn't always have a food truck on every corner. If a man wanted to eat well, he would be best served to make it himself." Dante stirred a bubbling pot of what looked like clam chowder on the stove. "I picked up a few tips from Rene Verdon when I worked for President Kennedy."

"That's not how I heard it." The director chuckled behind Rick. "Contemporary accounts say you spent more time in the White House kitchen than you did in the office."

"You know full well I was assigned to the President's detail after the Second World War. I had little reason to return to the office." Dante frowned and stared back at the pot of soup.

"PNI was founded as a branch of the FBI. J. Edgar Hoover demanded that Dante be assigned to him, rather than directly to the President like he had been for more than a century. Coolidge caved to his demands, as did every president Hoover ever faced off against." Director Leon scoffed as he led Rick back to the living room to sit. "To say they didn't get along would be putting it mildly. Dante despised Hoover – still does, as far as I can tell – and Hoover *hated* him. Office rumors couldn't decide if it was because Hoover made a pass at the boyish looking Dante and Dante turned him down, or if it was merely because Dante couldn't be controlled. Either way, Hoover made Dante's life a living nightmare. So much so, that when Dante enlisted after Pearl Harbor, Hoover had him assigned to the amphibious First Infantry Division."

The problems of Dante being involved in an amphibious assault didn't need to be explained. Rick frowned. Short of putting Dante in a submarine, he couldn't think of a less fitting assignment.

Director Leon gestured for Rick to take the La-Z-Boy while he took a seat on the couch. "Hoover pulled strings to make sure Dante was denied any medals, promotions, or recognition, even after Omaha. His name became legendary, however, and after the war he bonded with a young Massachusetts Congressman over their shared service. One of the first executive orders President Kennedy signed was to put PNI under the Secret Service." He leaned forward and lowered his voice. "Dante's convinced Hoover could have stopped the Kennedy assassination, and has never forgiven him for it. Rumor is that Dante never said a civil word to Hoover after that, and when informed that Hoover died, replied 'May God have mercy on his black soul.'"

"Rumors are not to be trusted, my friend." Dante scolded as he offered Rick a tray with a steaming bowl of soup and a rough slice of bread. "I actually said, 'Good riddance.' My partner at the time thought it was unseemly and spread the rumor you heard." He handed Director Leon his own tray. "And I don't believe I called you here to share decades old gossip. Today's events may rival those of that time if we do not act wisely."

"Catch me up." Director Leon sobered quickly. "I got Rick's text telling me the mythics were tired of the status quo and thought you were a traitor to the mythic race, and that if I didn't hear from you there was a real risk they would rise against the humans. Then an hour later, I got yours telling me to meet you here." He sipped the chowder from his spoon and gave Rick an evaluating look. "Though Dante's text indicated you were hurt."

"Not nearly as bad as I could have been. They were going to kill Dante and use me as part of some evil rite to keep him dead. Dante took out three of them in a terrible rage." Rick tasted his own soup and closed his eyes to savor it. It made the canned stuff taste like seawater and sand.

"Wharton and Laysha have more influence over the Council than is good for either mythics or humans." Dante sat next to Director Leon on the couch with his own bowl of soup. "I would have destroyed them all if Rick hadn't intervened. He discovered the link in the murders."

Director Leon froze with his slice of bread halfway to his mouth. "A link? My research team was convinced there wasn't one."

"They're all humans connected to mythics, apparently killed by mythics who had alibis." Rick made a sour face. "I probably wouldn't have figured it out if I hadn't nearly been one of them. And if I hadn't seen first hand the effect that framing the mythics could have on human mythic relationships."

"Someone is trying to start a war, Charles." Dante gestured with his spoon. "The question isn't who has motive as much as who acted on it."

"I'll see if I can get the FBI to help on the human side of things, see if they've heard anything other than from your stalker." The director gave Dante a stern look. "If you don't deal with Lynch, I will. I have scarier guys than you on the payroll."

"Yes, yes, he's my problem. I will deal with him." Dante frowned at Rick. "As soon as my partner is well enough to accompany me."

"Make Ciccarelli your second stop. The sniper that took out Dante was one of his. Coroner finally ID'd him." Director Leon shrugged. "Whether you'll get Chick to admit to it is anybody's guess."

"I have a few mythic contacts who are not members of the Council and may have a better feel for the sentiment on the ground." Dante stood and collected the empty trays. "The harpies like to gossip. It's possible they've heard something Vikas missed."

"Or didn't wish to share." Rick rubbed his side and stretched. "It's not like he was that cooperative today." He winced as he stood. The painkillers and food were helping, but what he really needed was to sleep until Christmas. "Well, I doubt the war is waiting for our schedule, so we probably should get started."

Dante laid a hand on his shoulder and pushed him back into the chair. "The war will not start this night, and Lynch is sure to be around whenever we want him. If you allow yourself to succumb to your injuries, I will likely be forced to return and finish what I started in the Guild house today."

"I'll send Agents Milton and Eliot to question the harpies. You're not the only one with contacts. And Dante, let's try not to provoke the Mythic Council if at all possible." Director Leon stood to go. "Rick, take care of yourself, for the good of the case. I shouldn't need to tell you that Dante burning down the Guild house will not end well for anyone."

"You two are terrible." Rick grumbled. "I'm not going to kill myself if I get out of this chair."

"Ah, but if you do not leave the chair, we can be sure of it." Dante chuckled and punched him lightly in the shoulder. "It is already dark. Lynch and Chick can wait until morning."

Chapter Nineteen

Rick was on the phone with his girlfriend when Dante went past his room on the way to the bathroom, and was *still* on the phone when he finished. Whatever problems the couple had had before he'd been injured seemed to have been easily worked out in the time since. Dante had meant what he'd told the girl – relationships were worth fighting for. Unfortunately, the secrets and danger involved in being his partner tended to put a strain on his partners' relationships. He prayed that Rick and Gracie's could survive the pressure.

While Rick showered, Dante made them breakfast. Rick's recovery had been cut short by Dante's inability to handle his own problems. The least he could do was make sure that Rick was cared for as much as possible. He set a plate of fried eggs, sausage, and toast alongside Rick's pain medication. Taking his partner out today was unavoidable. Perhaps managing the circumstances wasn't.

Rick rolled his eyes at the bottle of pills, but didn't comment as he ate his breakfast, took his pills, and pocketed the bottle for later.

"So how do we find Lynch?" Rick asked as they left the house.

"Funny thing, I have never actually *wanted* to find him before. Usually he finds me on his own." Dante smoothed his suit, a powder blue double breasted jacket with white embroidery on the cuffs and lapels. "But Charles sent me his address and the paperwork to file a restraining order."

"You know he's been in your house, right?" Rick pulled up the copy he'd made and turned the screen to Dante.

"*Mince.*" Dante paled and snatched the phone from Rick's hand. "Perhaps it is best if you manage this interview. I will be busy filling out the paperwork and trying not to murder him."

"Yeah, maybe don't say that too loudly. The last thing we need is another kangaroo court tribunal." Rick took his phone back and Dante watched as he emailed a copy of that video and the one of Wes Azusa's murder to Director Leon.

Furious that such a video even existed, Dante wasn't able to keep the venom from his voice as he replied, "If any mythics cared about Lynch, he would not be harassing me." He shrugged in disgust. "No, only humans would care about him, and you are easier to handle."

"You don't think he's behind the murders?" Rick rounded his Jeep and motioned for Dante to get in the passenger side.

"If it was solely an attack on you, perhaps. He's jealous that I didn't pick him to be my partner, but not a serial killer." Dante nudged an empty coffee cup aside with his foot, climbed in the car, and buckled up.

"Even if he decided to target *any* human partner of a mythic to get revenge for you rejecting him?" Rick's voice was quiet, but hard, and he rubbed his wounded side with his free hand.

"This is not my fault." Dante kept his voice level even as the Mythic Council's accusations echoed in his head. *He* blamed himself, even knowing it was ridiculous to do so, and it made him even more defensive than it should have.

"I'm not saying it is," Rick hastily amended. "Those idiots at the Guild House don't know what they're talking about. Making Lynch your partner would be incredibly stupid, and probably deadly, but he clearly doesn't think that. Could he retaliate by killing people who he thought got what he was denied?"

Dante considered for a moment. "Lynch is obnoxious, and might have accidentally incited one of his followers to violence, but I don't believe he has the courage to kill on his own, or the money to pay people to do it for him."

"You're probably right, but it sure would have made our lives easier." Rick turned to follow the phone's GPS instructions. "Have you ever been to his house before?"

"I try very hard to forget he exists." Dante scoffed. "But yes, once. He made a false report just to get me at his house. He tried to hit on Karyn – the 'tiny girl' Chick mentioned – and she kicked him in the teeth. Charles forwarded all his calls to DC Metro after that."

"So punching Lynch is a fantasy all your partners share, huh?" Rick pulled the Jeep up to a run-down bungalow on a street that hadn't seen better days in several decades. "How obnoxious does he have to be before I get a turn?"

"As much as I appreciate you punching Wharton earlier, let us try to limit aggression today to actual physical threats." Dante laughed. "I am sorry your sick leave was cut short, but I must confess I'm not sorry to have you by my side again."

They climbed the crumbling steps to the porch. Dante straightened his suit coat and preened his hair in the grimy reflection of the window beside the door, then knocked gingerly on the peeling wood of the screen door.

No answer. He opened the screen door and tried again on the front door while Rick rounded the house looking to see if there was any sign he was there.

A couple minutes later, the door unlocked, and a sullen-looking Lynch cracked open the door. Rick stood behind him with his arms crossed.

"Dante. I didn't expect you."

"We all know that's not true. I haven't done anything in eight years that you haven't known about." Dante pulled his PNI badge from the inside pocket of his coat. "You probably already know why we're here."

"I didn't attack your partner. I have an alibi." Lynch didn't look really happy to admit that.

"Let me guess. You were filming Dante at the time." Rick grunted.

Lynch nodded miserably. "I have it all on my phone. From the moment he gets the call, to him finding your body in that garage." He cued up a video on his phone and turned the screen to face Dante. "I was really excited to share it with my fans... until I realized I might be a suspect."

Seeing his own reaction to Rick's call was surreal, but he had absolutely no interest in reliving the moment he found his partner's bleeding body. Dante turned the phone away and pushed it back toward Lynch. "We're going to need an alibi for *all* the murders Rick and I have investigated since he came to PNI and access to your financials to make sure you didn't pay someone to do it for you."

"You can watch any of the videos I have, but you'll need a warrant for the financials." Lynch let a grey-faced Rick finish the video Dante had pushed away, then tapped to another one. "I know my rights."

Rick pushed the phone away as well. He cleared his throat twice before he could speak again. "We'll have you come down to the office to turn in the videos and make a statement. We saw the one you posted attempting to inflame humans against mythics."

"Hey, I wasn't inflaming anyone. It was all for the views. That video alone got the attention of a big sponsor."

"We're going to need the name of the sponsor, as well as anyone who reacted to your recent videos with threats of violence." Dante wondered how long the list was going to be. The internet seemed to bring out the lunatics more than any other invention in his considerable lifetime.

"I made a list to – ah – deflect suspicion when you guys came calling on me." He nodded toward the interior of the house. "Come on in and I'll get it."

"I don't think that's a great idea," Rick said, from his place already inside the house. "I'll go with him to get it and bring it out."

Lynch smirked at Rick. "Jealous, Agent McCoy?"

Rick laughed aloud. "Not of you. Not in a million lifetimes."

"I am not leaving you alone with my partner, no matter your alibi." Dante pushed the door open and gestured for Lynch to lead the way.

"I caught him heading out the back and brought him back through." Rick fell into step beside Dante, but never took his eyes off Lynch as he crossed into the kitchen and started sorting through a disorganized mass of papers on the table. "Also, don't say I didn't warn you."

Dante caught his breath and froze as they entered the living room. The house was filthy, yes, with dust, dirty laundry, and half-filled paper plates crawling with bugs scattered throughout the room, but that wasn't what caught Dante's eye. Every inch of bare wall space was covered with photos of him – some at the office, some through the windows of his own home, some at crime scenes, none with his permission. Cheap shelves attached to the walls were filled with small acrylic cases holding various items, labeled with embossed label tape. A badge from his FBI days sat on one shelf, far older than the period Lynch had been stalking him. Another acrylic box contained a plaster cast of the sole of Dante's Oxfords labeled "From the scene of the Mud Man Murders." He gave a high-pitched cry at the sight of a display labeled "Dante's glove" containing an ash stained kid glove.

"How much time will I get for punching him in the face?" Rick asked as he read a news article featuring a redacted version of Wes's death. "I'm trying to decide if it's worth it."

"Not nearly as long as I would for burning this abominable place to the ground." Dante gritted his teeth as he brushed aside mouse droppings to open the case and retrieve his glove. He remembered losing it, four years ago when he'd dropped it wrestling a naiad that had tried to take Wes to her lair. He'd barely survived that one, and the glove had been forgotten until after he and Wes were safe and the naiad returned to the nymph queen for judgment. "He's not worth it. He's a coward and an annoyance, but not worth jail time."

"A decade of harassment, theft, and privacy invasion is definitely worth it." Rick grumbled as Lynch came back from the kitchen clutching a stack of papers.

"Here's the screen shots of all the suspicious responses I got. I don't know who any of these people are, just their screen names." Lynch stuffed the papers into Rick's hands and glared at the glove Dante held.

"Say anything about the glove and I will take my chances with the DA," Rick snarled.

Lynch snapped his mouth shut and nodded.

"We have people at PNI that can trace the screen names." Dante scanned the room for anything else of his he might want back. Satisfied there was nothing in this room, and having no desire to check out any of the other rooms, he turned to go. "I recommend you go straight to the office and give your statement, or else I'll send a team from DC Metro to collect you and anything they feel is relevant to the case."

Lynch nodded emphatically with a pale face.

"And *I'll* arrest you myself if I see you hanging around any of our cases again." Rick gestured to the wall. "You have a problem. Get counseling."

Back at the car, Dante gingerly placed the soiled glove on the dashboard and brushed the filth from Lynch's house from his clothes and gloves.

"Ha, for once I feel the same way." Rick reached for a bottle of hand sanitizer sitting in the dash tray and used it generously. "At least we got what we came for." He shuffled through the crumpled and food stained papers. "His sponsor was a guy named Chad Faircloth. The rest of these are just names like 'mythic mesmer' and 'phoenix phantasies.' One of them, 'dante_dies_at_dawn,' gets pretty vocal."

Dante curled his lip in disgust. Were there more people out there obsessed with his life? Of course there were, or Lynch wouldn't have a following. "I don't want to know. Let's get this to the office and get real names and addresses we can follow up on. Meanwhile, I'm going to shower and burn my clothes."

"Dry cleaning is cheaper." Rick laughed as he threw the car into gear. "I'm beginning to wonder how you're not buying knockoffs from shady websites at the rate you go through clothes."

At Dante's indignant look, Rick amended quickly, "I'm teasing – sort of. Burning your clothes on purpose *is* a bit bombastic, and wasteful."

"I suppose. I won't really burn them." Dante picked a stray mouse turd off his cuff and gagged. "As much as I may want to."

Chapter Twenty

The office identified "dante_dies_at_dawn" as the same man that had sponsored Lynch's Cryptid Conspiracies channel. Chad Faircloth ran a private agricultural credit union in town and had given Lynch three thousand dollars to advertise his bank on the next stream. He lived outside Fairfax in a farmhouse with solar panels and a tall privacy fence. The front yard was planted with corn instead of grass, obscuring most of the house, and a diesel Ford F-150 sat in the driveway.

"I'll bet his neighbors love him." Rick eyed the perfectly landscaped yard next door as he parked behind the pickup truck.

Dante looked from the neatly trimmed grass to the shoulder-height corn with a look of sheer confusion.

"Don't tell me you've never seen a corn lawn before?" Rick barked a sharp laugh, more amused by Dante's reaction than the lawn itself. "My parents' neighbors in Indiana did this one summer, drove them nuts, but at least he stopped mowing the lawn in his underwear."

"Please don't tell me this is a common thing." Dante narrowed his eyes at him like he thought he was teasing him.

"I mean, apparently not as common as vampires in DC, but yeah, it's a thing." Rick looked again at his partner suspiciously. The flamboyant agent wore a Lacoste polo shirt and a pair of Ralph Lauren khakis. "What are you wearing?"

"The man goes by 'dante_dies_at_dawn.' You are correct, I cannot afford to keep losing suits like this." His face flushed with embarrassment. "Please do not say anything to Charles. Or Lynch. Or Ravinia." The redness in Dante's face faded to a greenish gray. "If you say anything about this to anyone, I will cast myself into the Potomac."

Rick focused ahead of him and coughed twice to keep from breaking up into laughter. "Let's try to avoid getting shot at in the first place." Honestly, Rick wasn't certain why they were sent to question a guy who clearly had it in for mythics in general and his partner specifically, other than PNI's flippant reliance on Dante's resurrection ability to cover for otherwise sketchy situations. "You realize if we were both human, they wouldn't let us within five hundred feet of this place."

"Then it is a good thing one of us is not human, no?" Dante shrugged off his former embarrassment and took the lead up to the door.

Dante knocked, waited, then knocked again. After the second time, someone peeked through the blinds covering the window beside the door. Rick shoved his badge against the glass and the face disappeared. A moment later, the door cracked open, held to only a couple inches by at least four chains.

"I shoot salesmen." The guy inside shoved the barrel of a sawed off shotgun through the crack.

"I'm Agent Rick McCoy and this is my partner." Rick cut off Dante before he could say his name. Better the guy didn't flip out immediately. "I know you saw my badge. Open the door, we have questions for you."

"I know my rights." The man grunted as he pulled the door closed and started undoing chains.

"You're absolutely right. You don't have to talk to us. That's fine." Rick rolled his eyes. "Except, well, that shotgun you're waving around is illegal. We can make it official and read you your Miranda rights and take this to the office."

"Fine, make it quick." Faircloth swung the door open, but didn't aim the gun away from them. He bobbed the gun barrel at Dante. "I thought *you'd* show up eventually. I'm prepared. Loaded it with bird shot."

"Are you serious?" Dante rolled his eyes and gestured to himself. "Do I look like a bird to you?"

"Maybe not in those clothes." Rick made a short laugh through his nose. "Your regular outfit *does* make you look a little like a peacock."

Dante gave him a withering look.

"VampirePhoenix said..." Faircloth hesitated and lowered his rifle a little, but raised it quickly as soon as Rick made a move toward him. "It doesn't matter. Hurts like heck whatever you are." He swung it to point at Rick. "And what *are* you?"

"Human, same as you." He kept his hands up and visible as he took a careful step closer and to the left. If they spread out a bit, he couldn't cover both of them. "I can show you my badge again if you let me pull it from my pocket."

"I ain't got a problem with cops." He gestured with a thumb behind him at a sticker in his front window of a black and white flag with a blue line through it. "Just with weirdos."

"Well, you got us there. Agent Brand is definitely a weirdo." Rick ignored the indignant sound Dante made and kept going, drawing closer to the angry man as he did. "Does it make a difference that he's one of the *good* weirdos? Even VampirePhoenix's channel can tell you that."

Faircloth considered that for a moment. "The only good weirdo is a dead weirdo." He raised his gun to point at Dante's chest.

Rick wedged himself between the barrel of the gun and his partner, ignoring Dante's low protest and the pounding of his own heart. Faircloth knew shooting Dante would cause no permanent damage, and so had no reason to hesitate over pulling the trigger apart from the risk of damage to his own front porch. A human target was a different story, and one Rick prayed would give the other man pause. "Is that how it went down with the waitress and the yacht owner? Did you kill them because you wanted everyone to hate the mythics as much as you do?"

"What? No, I didn't kill anyone!" Faircloth stabbed his breastbone with the shotgun.

Dante cleared his throat and reached around Rick to grab the barrel of the gun with his bare hand, melting it into an unusable puddle of metal. "Seeing the way you wave that around, you'll have to pardon us if we don't take your word for it. You *do* have an alibi, I hope?"

Faircloth looked at the mangled gun dumbfounded. "How would I know?" he finally responded sullenly. "I don't even know what dates I need an alibi for."

Dante pulled on his glove and listed the dates and times of the murders they suspected were connected.

"My wife can vouch for the ones that happened over night." Faircloth jabbed a thumb at the house behind him. "My partner out at the credit union can testify for the others."

An interview with his wife didn't lead to anything more than an angry tirade about all Faircloth ever did was work, sleep, and chat on social media with his doomsday friends. Somewhere in that load of bile, Rick and Dante gathered that the couple had been fighting during a couple of the murders, and that Faircloth had been at work for a couple more. After a goodbye that neither member of the couple seemed to hear, Rick and Dante left for the credit union.

"Don't you ever do that again." Dante said softly once they were back at the car.

It took Rick a moment of mental scrambling to figure out exactly what "that" was. "Talk down a homicidal hillbilly? Keep you from getting killed again?"

"Step between me and a threat." Dante clenched a gloved fist.

"He wasn't going to shoot me. He didn't want to go to prison for shooting a human cop. *I* was in no danger. He clearly had it in for you, though." Rick curled his lip as the graphic memories of the three times Dante had died already since he took the job played in his head and turned his stomach. "I don't care if you *do* resurrect, it's still horrible watching you die. I don't know how any of your partners become jaded enough to just let themselves ignore that feeling."

"Most don't." Dante sighed. "And those that do lose something of their humanity in the process." He shook his head as if at an unpleasant memory, and added with a hard voice, "It doesn't change the fact that I *do* resurrect, and you do not. If one of us is going to die, it simply has to be me."

"And if neither of us *has* to die, how about we don't?" Rick shrugged. "Saves us both a lot of hassles. You're welcome to take a bullet for me if it's unavoidable, but maybe we both look for ways to keep from coming into contact with them in the first place."

"That is fair." Dante laughed. "Dying is only an unpleasant interruption for me, I forget sometimes that it is traumatic to those forced to observe it."

Rick grunted. "That would be an incredible understatement, but we'll go with that."

A chime from Dante's pocket had him reaching for his phone.

"As I thought, Lynch didn't have the resources to pay for a hit man." Dante read from his phone. "Faircloth's financials are a bit less clear. He has multiple unusual large expenditures."

"Probably investing in a doomsday bunker in Kansas." Rick scoffed as he pulled into a parking spot at the credit union.

"That's on here, too. Partner's name is– *Mince!*" Dante slammed the phone against his lap. "Shamus Finnegan."

"Oooh-kay?" Rick took a deep breath. "Let me guess, he's a leprechaun."

"The king of the leprechauns, actually."

"My first question is, does Faircloth know?" Rick started laughing. "Can you imagine a mythic being *working* with that guy every day?"

"It does seem like it would be unpleasant, yes." Dante frowned. "He was on the council."

"The short guy who stood up for you?"

"Umm Hmm."

"That shouldn't be a problem, then. He'll be more disposed to cooperate with us than a werewolf or vampire." Rick opened his door and climbed out.

"Suspecting an ally's partner of murder is not a great look." Dante rounded the trunk and pulled his spare suit coat out of his duffel bag, and shrugged it on. It was black with bright yellow embroidery that complimented his polo shirt. "We must tread lightly."

"You'd better ask the questions, then." Rick bowed mockingly for Dante to lead the way. "We don't have a lot of mythic allies left."

"More than you think, but yes, we should be careful." Dante smoothed his coat, tugged at his gloves, and set his face toward the bank.

A cute blonde that looked as human as possible greeted them from behind the counter. "Good afternoon, gentlemen. Can I help you?"

"Yes." Dante smiled at her brightly as he showed her his badge. "We're with the Secret Service. We need to ask Mr. Finnegan a few questions."

Her smile faltered. "I hope there's no trouble?"

"I don't expect there to be Miss Tiffany." Dante waved a gloved hand carelessly. "Just a few simple questions, and we'll be gone. You can tell him Agent Dante Brand and his partner are here."

Seeming somewhat appeased. The girl at the counter entered a side office for a moment, then came back to them. "Mr. Finnegan will see you."

They entered the banker's office to see a very short man with red hair and beard sitting in a raised chair behind a large desk. The office was richly decorated with brocade curtains, textured carpet, and a massive aquarium with tropical fish taking up the wall behind the banker's desk.

"Agent Brand, Agent McCoy." The leprechaun stood on his chair and leaned forward to extend his hand to Dante. "I hope there's no trouble?"

"We're just here to ask a couple questions about your partner." Dante took one of the seats opposite the desk and Rick followed suit.

"Oh, dear, what did he do now?" The leprechaun rolled his eyes to the ceiling.

"Maybe nothing worse than internet harassment." Rick shrugged. Being a jerk wasn't a crime, and Finnegan's reaction indicated he already knew his partner was that. "We're hoping you can fill in a couple gaps for us."

Dante gave the banker the dates and times Faircloth still needed alibis for, and the leprechaun relaxed.

"He was here. He's *always* here by then, and sometimes even sleeps on a Murphy bed in his office. You're welcome to check our security camera footage." The banker shrugged. "He's a blowhard, but I swear his bark is worse than his bite."

"He advertised the credit union on a video channel inciting war between mythics and humans. Has he ever used bank funds to further his views or in any other suspicious ways?" Dante asked gently.

"Not that I'm aware of." Finnegan stroked his beard thoughtfully. "I'll say though, I've handled a lot of odd loans lately from people looking to prepare for 'the worst' – not that *that's* particularly new – it's just gotten more frequent since the murders started. A lot of them are mythics or humans with mythic connections, like Giovanni Ciccarelli."

"Ciccarelli took out a loan? Did he say why?" Rick narrowed his eyes. The shady mobster being involved wouldn't surprise him in the least.

"Officially, for capital improvements on the club." The banker shrugged. "But he kept hinting that there was a deeper reason and implied *I* should know what it was."

"And why should you know what it was?" Rick glanced over to see Dante's grim expression. Chick just climbed up the suspects list to the top.

"He laughed as he was leaving and said something I attributed at the time to his, ahem, less than savory reputation,'War loans are a very lucrative business, aren't they Mr. Finnegan.'"

Chapter Twenty-One

After lunch and a change of clothes for Dante, they returned to Ciccarelli's gym a little more warily than before. Not only did they have reason to suspect that Chick was behind the sniper that had taken Dante out at the fountain, Finnegan's statement seemed to indicate that Chick had known about the murders before they happened.

Dante had arrested Chick half a dozen times before, and Chick's father before him probably twice that many times, but nothing ever seemed to stick. He wasn't overly optimistic today would be different. He wasn't even entirely sure what they thought Chick was guilty of. Inciting war didn't seem like his style. Taking advantage of it, certainly, but their case was the killings and nothing connected him to those.

Dante adjusted his gloves and took a deep breath as he stepped out of Rick's jeep into the parking lot of Chick's gym and looked around warily. He really wasn't in the mood to be shot again.

"We're clear." Rick took his side with his gun drawn and ready. His grim expression indicated he was less than thrilled by the prospect of confronting Chick. "If that ugly werewolf alpha even looks at us funny, I'm shooting him in the face."

"Wharton would be a fool to oppose us again. We have beaten him twice, and PNI knows we're here. Chick's gym is not a protected space like the council." Dante frowned as uncertainty tugged at the back of his mind in spite of the confidence in his words. Not that Wharton wouldn't bluster. Getting beaten twice had to hurt his pride, and damaging a werewolf alpha's pride was an unforgivable offense.

"How does this work, exactly?" Rick holstered his gun but held his hand at the ready. "Does Wharton's behavior at the council implicate Ciccarelli?"

"No more than what you do in your spare time reflects on me." Dante opened the door and held it for his partner. "Contrary to what Laysha was trying to assert, no one owns or controls anyone else. There *are* exceptions, such as a vampire's thrall or a kitsune who loses his spirit ball, but those are rare in the modern mythic community."

"You say that as if they weren't so rare in the past." Rick curled his lip in disgust as they headed to Chick's office.

"Mythology exists for a reason." Dante laughed. After everything, Rick was still so skeptical. "Where did you think the stories came from?"

"Exaggeration? Hyperbole? Isolated incidents conflated into common occurrences. Basically the historical equivalent to everything on the internet." Rick eyed a kelpie in the form of a man with dreads and an Iktomi spider shifter in native paint sparring at one mat. "Okay, they look terrifying. When you fight here, do you actually win? Without burning the place down?"

"Quite often." Dante chuckled. "It's the only reason Chick tolerates me."

Tolerate was not exactly the operative word today. When they entered Giovanni Ciccarelli's office, he was flanked by Wharton on one side and a massive human enforcer on the other and his expression was somewhat less than welcoming.

Dante glanced over at Rick, and clenched his teeth against the temptation to order his partner back to the car. Wharton's toothy grin nearly guaranteed that this was going to get ugly.

"Don't even think about it," Rick murmured out of the side of his mouth as he pushed past Dante into the office and flashed his badge at the trio. "We're here on official business. You can make it easy and answer our questions here, or we can all go down to the office and do it there. I'm tired of inhaling smoke and would rather do this without my partner needing to burn things, but that's also entirely up to you."

"Dante, when have I been anything less than cooperative?" Chick feigned a hurt expression as he leaned heavily on his arm brace crutch, rounded the desk, and gave Dante a rough hug with his free arm. "You know you're always welcome here. Maybe we can even set up a bout between you and Wharton here. People'd pay big bucks to see you two go at it."

"Thank you, Chick, not today." Dante inclined his head to Wharton. "Though I think such a match is inevitable."

Wharton snarled at Dante and bared his teeth, causing Rick and the human enforcer to tense. The office was small and humans were absolutely going to die if they fought here.

Dante pointedly turned his focus to Chick. "One of your enforcers shot me, twice. We need to know if he was acting under your orders."

"You know I'd far rather see you beaten in a fair fight that's making me money than paying money to have one of my men take pointless potshots at you." Chick rolled his eyes. "Besides, I've had plenty of opportunities to off you in the past, and you're still here. You're barking up the wrong tree. What motive would I have to kill you now?"

"Perhaps your motive was warning us away from investigating your son." Rick offered tightly, his wary eyes watching the enforcer's hands. "Or to prevent us from finding out about your war prep loans."

"We all know Giuceppe is innocent and Vikas told Wharton and a couple other members of the council to be prepared for when things go south. To make sure they're ready for the inevitable war with the humans. Wharton faithfully passed the advice on to me." Chick swore. "If prepping were a crime, a quarter of Maryland would be under suspicion. You want to inspect my garden for clues next, Brand?"

"Did Vikas say how he knew things were going 'south' now after peace for so long?" Rick looked at Chick's human enforcer again and moved his hand to his gun.

Dante narrowed his eyes and tried to see what his partner saw, but Chick was between them and other than the enforcer's tense posture and unyielding stare that never left Rick's face Dante saw nothing. Chick had never ordered his men to hurt one of Dante's partners, but Dante wasn't interested in allowing harm to come to Rick simply because it hadn't happened *yet*. He ran a finger under the edge of his right glove as subtly as possible. Still, Wharton's gaze flicked to Dante's hands and the werewolf curled his lip in a silent, but no less threatening snarl. Dante opened his hands and let them drop to his side. *Holy God, protect us.*

Chick barked a sharp laugh and answered Rick's question as if nothing strange was going on in the background. "War is always on the verge of happening, Agent McCoy. Nobody needs to be a prophet to see that."

"Would you ever have cause to *provoke* that war, Chick?" Dante asked softly, his eyes on Wharton.

"Provoke? Of course not, but I have every intention of being on the right side – whatever side that may be." Chick gestured to his enforcers. "Vikas has personally made it clear that you're on the wrong one, Agent Brand. He's placed a bounty on your head that will more than make up for the loss your death will have on my profits."

"You may find collecting on that bounty more costly than you anticipate, Chick." Dante went for his glove, as the massive human enforcer went for his gun and aimed it at Rick. A split second decision sent him diving to protect his partner as the enforcer fired. Dante managed to knock Rick to the floor out of the way, but a searing pain ripped through his own side.

He hit the ground with a cry and clutched a gloved hand to his wounded side. It came back dark with his own blood. The room tipped and his hair fell into his face as he pressed his hands to the floor as he tried to steady himself. He'd died enough times to recognize a mortal wound. He didn't have long.

"Rick?" He gasped in pain as he dragged himself to where his partner lay against the wall.

His partner didn't move, didn't respond. Fear clutched at Dante's chest. He'd taken the bullet, why wasn't Rick all right?

"Take them out and dispose of the bodies in a way that our phoenix friend won't be making a comeback." Chick ordered his enforcers. "Make it fast. That wound looks bad. You don't want to be near Agent Brand when he dies."

Dante tried to shift his weight so he could pull off his gloves and defend Rick at the very least, but his legs and arms shook so badly he collapsed beside his partner instead. *Gracious God, preserve us.*

Wharton grabbed him around the waist and threw him over his shoulder like a sack, taking no care to avoid contact with Dante's wound. Pain shot through Dante's body when he bumped it, making him scream and his consciousness fade. He had to stay awake. If he passed out now, his resurrection fire would take out all three of the others. He had to remain conscious at least until Rick woke up and could defend himself.

If he woke up. *Mince!* Why wasn't Rick awake? The massive human enforcer scooped his partner up like a baby and he didn't even stir. Dante could only think that he'd hit his head as he went down, an injury that was about to become every bit as fatal as if he *had* been shot.

Chick's enforcers hauled them through a back door to a rundown shed in the back. They dumped them roughly on the ground as they dragged something from the shed and set it in the back of a pickup truck. Dante rolled over with some difficulty and crawled the three feet to his partner's side. Even that much effort left him panting for breath and sweating. He laid a gloved hand on Rick's chest and was relieved to find that it rose and fell steadily. He shook Rick's shoulder, then punched him in the arm with all the strength he could muster. Rick groaned and stirred, but didn't awaken.

"Hey, now! None of that." Wharton kicked him in the side and dragged him by his wrists toward the truck.

The sharp pain made Dante vomit on himself and lose consciousness for a moment. He came to when he hit the bottom of a mildewed casket. Pain spread though his abdomen and the sky spun overhead so much he felt like throwing up again. If Rick's safety hadn't been in question, he'd welcome death. His suit was a loss anyway.

"Chick had this built for Vizzini back when they were feuding. He didn't get the opportunity to use it. Unfortunately for you." Wharton gave him a toothy grin and jiggled a lock hasp. "It locks and the base is layered with cement. You and your latest loser are done, Brand."

A shadow clouded Dante's vision and Rick's body landed awkwardly on top of his. Panic staved off unconsciousness as Wharton leaned on the casket lid to force it closed over them. Dante squirmed to try to free his hands, but didn't have the strength to do more than cause himself more pain and speed exsanguination. He needed Rick's help, or they were both dead.

He wavered between consciousness and death as the truck sped jauntily away from the gym. He was vaguely aware at one point that the casket was moved to a boat. At least, the unsteadiness he felt became more like the familiar motion of rough water and muffled noises sounded like the docks. He took slow, deep breaths to fight for the last bits of clarity he could muster. He didn't have long before he died, and in these close quarters his resurrection fire would kill his friend. As the casket lurched into the water with a dull splash, he wondered if it was already too late.

Chapter Twenty-Two

Rick woke up with a throbbing headache that felt like his own brain was attacking him. He groaned and tried to move, but silk pressed against him on every side. On three sides, it was the firm, silk covered interior of a casket. Beneath him was Dante's silk-shirted torso, warm and slick with blood. His partner's chest rose and fell with shallow, uneven breaths. The air in the casket was stale with the overwhelming metallic smell of blood and rotten smells of mildew and vomit making it hard to breathe. Snatches of memory made their way past the drum solo in his head.

Dante had tackled him and taken the shot meant for him. Rick must have hit his head on the way down, and Dante clearly didn't die – yet anyway.

"Dante?" Rick tried to scoot off his wounded partner as far as he could to give him space to breathe. A horrible thought occurred to him: what if they were buried in the casket? How much oxygen did a casket even hold? He pushed at the lid, but it didn't budge.

"Rick? Thank God you're awake." Dante's voice was little more than a raspy whisper. "We have to get you out of here. There's not much time."

"Right. There can't be much oxygen in here. Especially not for both of us."

"No, I..." Dante took a shaky breath. His voice hitched as he continued, "If you're not clear when I die, I will kill you."

Rick's blood ran cold. "How long are we talking here?"

"I cannot tell, but it isn't long... I feared you wouldn't awaken in time." Dante's voice trailed off and his breathing became more shallow, so much so that Rick had to lay a panicked hand on his partner's chest to feel him breathe.

Rick punched Dante in the arm as hard as their cramped situation allowed. Dante took a gasping breath and fumbled with something in his hand.

"Keep this for me." Dante pressed his rosary into Rick's hand. "And help me get my glove off, I can't get my other hand free." He held up a shaky hand while Rick gingerly pulled his glove off. "I was conscious when they dumped us... mostly. I'm pretty sure they dumped the coffin in the Potomac, rather than burying it." He wheezed a short laugh, that turned into a fit of coughing. "Apparently they were more concerned about quenching my fire than actually keeping you from escaping. Which means if I can burn open the lid, you'll have a shot at the surface."

Rick frowned. There were a lot of problems with Dante's plan. The Potomac varied *vastly* in depth, and the strong current actually made it so dangerous that swimming in it was against the law. *If* Dante could burn through enough of the lid before the water put out his fire, and *if* Rick could get to the top before he ran out of oxygen himself, he'd still have the challenge of finding his partner's body. It was a long shot, Dante had to know that, so Rick worked the rosary into the pocket of his pants and said nothing. *Jesus, help us here.*

And they that know thy name will put their trust in thee: for thou, Lord, hast not forsaken them that seek thee. A verse of Scripture and a completely irrational sense of peace filled his heart.

"You can swim, right?" Dante froze with one hand half an inch from the silk covered lid.

"You know that probably won't make a difference, right?" Rick focused on taking deep breaths to get all the oxygen he could in his bloodstream before he hit the water.

"I am sorry, my friend." Dante glanced at the glove still in Rick's hand. "You can give that back when you come back for me."

"Lord willing." Rick awkwardly stuffed the glove in his pocket with the rosary and sighed. "Let's do this."

"Gracious God, in the name of your Holy Son, I ask that you grant my partner his life." Dante made a quick gesture and focused the flames in his hands at the lid, softly muttering a prayer in Latin as he worked. Smoke immediately filled the small space, making it impossible to breathe. Rick held his breath and squeezed his eyes shut. If he didn't get out soon, he'd use up his oxygen before he even hit the water.

Dante's flame flickered and failed, his hands falling to his side and the rise and fall of his chest stilling.

Panic grabbed Rick by the throat as he automatically started Dante's resurrection countdown. Thirty seconds. If he wasn't free in thirty seconds, they were both dead.

Dante had managed to burn away the lid deep into the wood, leaving charred walnut and strips of singed silk. Rick prayed it was enough to weaken the lid, and kicked it with all his might.

The lid splintered, letting water stream through the cracks, but held. Rick's chest already ached, and certainty that he wasn't even going to make it out of the casket before he ran out of air nagged at the corners of his mind. He hit the lid again, this time with his knees and fists. It gave, flooding the casket and ending the threat of Dante's resurrection fire. With a silent promise to return for his friend, Rick pushed free of the casket and shot toward the surface.

Please, let us be above the falls. Most of the Potomac averaged twenty-four feet deep, but the tidal area south of the falls could get more than a hundred feet deep. Not only would he not make it to the surface, both his and Dante's bodies would wash out to sea long before anyone found them.

His lungs burned and his body ached. Dante was counting on him. He had to come back for his partner. Blackness edged his vision. The iron cross of Dante's rosary dug into his thigh from inside his pocket, reminding him that he wasn't alone.

Jesus, give me the strength to get to the top. Rick's head broke the surface and he sucked in a deep gasp of air, treading water as he tried to catch his breath and get his bearings. He needed to get to the shore and call the director to help rescue Dante. Trees lined either side of the river. Getting out wasn't going to be the problem. Getting back to civilization with a waterlogged phone might be. How far were they from DC? Rick hadn't exactly had an opportunity to explore much since he'd moved.

His side began to ache and he gritted his teeth against the pain. He needed to get to shore and then figure it out. Struggling against the current as little as possible, he struck out diagonally toward the bank and pulled himself out of the water. He leaned back against a tree and held his arm to his side as he struggled to catch his breath. His side cramped and he curled around his still healing wound with a low cry. Hiking out of the woods to civilization was out of the question. *Dear Jesus, we're not out of the woods yet. I have no idea where I am, much less how to get Dante's body back. I'm going to need your help here.*

As he finished praying, a couple in a paddle boat rounded a bend in the river. With a teary laugh, he shouted and waved. "Hey! I need a little help here."

The couple looked at him startled, then at each other nervously. For a terrifying moment he was afraid they were going to paddle by, but they slowly turned toward him and waved back.

"How did you get out here?" The man shouted back at him as they paddled closer.

Rick worked his soggy wallet out of his saturated pants and showed them his badge. "I'm a Federal agent. My case went sour and the bad guy dumped me and my partner in the Potomac."

The couple's skeptical looks turned horrified and they paddled harder toward him.

"Where's your partner?" The man offered him a hand and helped him onto the back of the paddle boat while scanning the woods.

Rick hesitated. There was *no* way he was going to explain that in a way that wouldn't freak them out. "We got separated. If I can call my boss, he can get a team out here to look for my partner."

The woman nodded enthusiastically, tapped the screen of her phone a couple times and handed it to him.

"Thanks, uh, where are we?" Rick tapped in the digits of Director Leon's number and held the phone to his ear.

"Just north of Fletcher's Cove." The couple started paddling back out into the river. "You can tell your boss to meet us there."

"Director Charles Leon, PNI?" Director Leon answered after only one ring. "This is a private line. How did you get this number?"

"Director, it's Rick McCoy. I need a recovery team to meet me at Fletcher's Cove." Rick kept his voice low as he tried to code the conversation as much as possible. "Dante and I were dumped into the Potomac."

"Dante's still down there?" Director Leon sounded grim, but he clearly understood the problem. "Did he die before he hit the water? Did you mark where he went down?"

"Yes, and roughly. I was kind of with him." Rick looked out into the river and frowned. As long as Dante's body stayed in the casket, finding him should be easy. If he somehow drifted free, they may never find him. Fear gripped Rick's stomach. "We're at Fletcher's Cove."

"I'll bring a team and some paramedics. I'll need a full report when I get there." Director Leon hung up.

Rick handed the phone back to the couple who then made small talk about his job all the way to the dock. By the time they left him alone sitting on the dock, his head was pounding and his side ached. Sirens neared and two ambulances, three MPD patrol cars, and the director's black sedan careened into the parking lot. The uniformed officers swept through and herded the civilians behind the vehicles while the director and a pair of paramedics approached him. Rick lifted his head from his hands and waved the paramedics off.

"I need to know if you're going to collapse on me, Rick." The director gave him an assessing look, his eyes lingering on the fading blood stains on his clothes.

"I have a concussion and my side is on fire." Rick stood and gritted his teeth against the pain and dizziness. "But the blood is Dante's and I'm not going anywhere until I have him back."

Chapter Twenty-Three

The director pressed his lips in a tight line and dismissed the paramedics. "I have a recovery vessel enroute. I need the whole story."

"We confronted Ciccarelli, and he tried to have us killed. Dante took a bullet meant for me and I hit my head. When I woke up, we were at the bottom of the Potomac in a rotting casket. Dante helped me get free before he died, but I'm pretty sure the casket flooded when I escaped. There's no way he could have resurrected, and I think there's a good chance he's still in the casket."

"That'd make life easier for all of us." The director stared off into the river. "Pray that we find him, Rick, without having to drag the whole river."

They got onboard the recovery vessel and Rick pointed out where he reached the surface. The strength of the current meant that they needed to start looking significantly farther up river.

"Director Leon, Agent McCoy." The captain of the cutter, a thin, weathered looking man with a painted shell on a cord around his neck frowned at them. "There's no chance he's *alive* is there?"

Both of them looked at Rick. He shook his head. "Not whatsoever. I'm pretty sure he was dead before I got free, but even if he wasn't, the water took care of that long ago." He stuffed his hands in his pockets to hide the fact that they had started shaking. It had been easy enough to ignore the reality of what happened when he had been focused on survival and *rescue,* but the reality was that he'd watched his partner die, *again.* They were treating this as a *recovery*, rather than a rescue. The fact that Dante *might* resurrect after they recovered his body was the only thing keeping Rick from melting down now. His fingertips brushed the crucifix on Dante's rosary. *Jesus, let us rescue him.*

Director Leon gave him an evaluating look. "Steady, Agent McCoy."

Rick gave his boss a deadly look, and barely refrained from making a sharp comment or flat out punching his boss in the teeth. "I've been stabbed, shot at, concussed, and buried at sea. My partner took a bullet and bled out beside me, and you want me to just blow it off like he's napping or something. Pardon me if this is all just a bit much."

"I shouldn't have to tell you why I'm not thrilled to have you two on my boat." The captain gestured at them. "And no mythic captain in his right mind wants Brand near his boat *alive,* never mind *dead.* Boats and fire are a terrible combination."

"Once we locate him by sonar, recovery divers are going to put him in a special body bag underwater." Director Leon assured him, "All you need to do is tow him back to Fletcher's Cove. Agent McCoy and I will make sure he's taken care of from there."

The captain gave a dissatisfied grunt, but went back to navigating his crew down the Potomac. Director Leon motioned for Rick to follow him to the rail at the bow of the boat, where they leaned to watch the crews work.

"I was the one Dante mentioned as having fished him out of Lake Michigan after a case in Chicago went south." Director Leon stared off into the water as if remembering the case. "I'd forgotten how upset I was. I'd gotten used to seeing Dante resurrect by then, even from a few deaths so gruesome I try to block out the memory. But he was dead for a day and a half before we found him, and I was nearly beside myself. Everyone told me repeatedly that I had to clear the area for a resurrection after thirty seconds, but no one ever told me what would happen if the deadline passed without him resurrecting. I was tormented by the idea that it might be too late by the time we retrieved him. I also sort of assumed he couldn't resurrect under water, but then

I wondered if he'd spent the entire thirty seven and a half hours resurrecting only to drown immediately and repeat in thirty seconds. I nearly drove myself crazy trying to do that math. That's... a lot of very horrible dying."

"Is this supposed to make me feel better?" Rick gripped the rail with white knuckled hands as his own mind now grappled with the same questions.

"Let me finish." Director Leon raised a hand. "Dante resurrected thirty seconds after we got him dried out. He assured me he wasn't aware of anything after the first death, which, while horrible enough, was nothing like what my brain imagined him going through. I know it's terrible, watching him die. I forget that sometimes now that I'm not dealing with it on a daily basis. *He* forgets that, regularly, because it's literally a way of life for him." Director Leon frowned. "All that to say, we're going to find him, and he's going to be fine. The first thing he's going to do is demand you bring him his clothes. Yes, he's vain, but it's also his way of grounding himself and making sure you're unharmed in the process. He's woken up to find partners dead more times than I even know. If he can yell at you about his clothes, he knows you're alive."

Rick snorted. "Well, he's going to have to yell. His bag's in the trunk of my car in Ciccarelli's parking lot."

"I sent a team to arrest Chick, Wharton, and Benson. You and Dante can ID them officially when the paramedics clear you both. The team's also retrieving your car and Dante's clothes. They'll meet us at the cove before we get there."

"Is there anything you didn't think of?" Rick's teeth started chattering. Even though the afternoon sun was still warm, he was wet, cold and tired.

"Of course not, that's why I'm the director." Director Leon passed him a rough blanket and gave him a half smile. "Well, I may have forgotten food. I'll order pizza for the whole crew once we're done here."

Each pass across the river seemed to take an eternity, and Rick eventually found himself sitting on the deck with his back against the rail, his knees pulled to his chest, his arms folded on his knees, and his head resting on his arms. Director Leon checked on him every so often, to make sure his own condition wasn't deteriorating. After several passes, Rick was awakened by shouting and the director shaking his shoulder.

"Sonar spotted something. The divers are going down now."

Rick groaned and stretched. His body was stiff and sore from his injuries and position, so he used the rail to help him stand. The director frowned, but thankfully didn't say anything. Like "I'm calling the paramedics back" or "Get this man a stretcher." He leaned on the rail to watch the divers submerge where they were directed and stay down for what seemed like an eternity. Rick wasn't sure if that meant they found Dante and were preparing to bring him up, or if it meant the sonar had picked up some random object instead of his partner's casket, or if the swift current had pulled his partner's body downstream. After his own swim, he was well aware that could be a possibility – a possibility he prayed didn't materialize. The sun was already low on the horizon, and Rick doubted they would continue searching in the dark.

After a while, the divers' heads appeared above the surface of the river. One tugged on the tow line and waved to the captain.

"They've got him." Director Leon sounded as relieved as Rick felt. For all his confidence earlier, maybe he *had* been a little worried about his former partner and friend.

"Thank God." Rick spotted the black body bag dragging in the wake of the boat and laughed darkly. "Dante would have a fit if he knew we subjected him to the indignity of dragging him behind a boat."

Director Leon chuckled. "At least no one else can see him. We'll have that going in our defense."

"What's it going to take to get him awake?" Rick asked as they neared Fletcher's Cove. "It's been hours since he died. Rigor mortis... Does he experience rigor mortis?"

"Yes." The director's answer was quick and sharp, backed by his own memories of the last time. "He dies just like you or I. But *he* comes back." Director Leon looked at Rick grimly. "Once we get him ashore, we have to move fast. I don't want either of us caught in his resurrection blast, but if we don't get the wet clothes off him he might not resurrect. He has to burn, right?"

Director Leon didn't sound confident.

"You have no idea, do you?"

"None whatsoever." The director chuckled wryly. "No one really knows the mechanics of Dante's resurrection, not even him. I just know we want it to happen when we're nowhere near by. We also want the bullet that killed him as evidence if we can manage it. It's hard to convict a guy of murder when the victim not only is alive, but also destroyed all the evidence."

"You think you can get a bullet out in thirty seconds?"

"Guess we're going to find out."

The boat slowed and pulled close to the paddle boat dock. The divers quickly dragged Dante's body bag up on the beach, out of the water and away from the boat docks. The director waved them off as he and Rick disembarked onto the dock and scrambled toward the black form in the sand.

"It's go time, Agent McCoy." Director Leon crouched beside the bag and handed Rick a heavy pair of scissors. "We get him out of the bag and you start on his clothes. I'll retrieve the bullet. Twenty-five seconds and we both clear the resurrection radius. Got it?"

Rick nodded. The paramedics and civilians had cleared the beach hours ago, but the police line remained and gave them plenty of privacy to work. *Dear Jesus, let this work.* Somewhere in the back of his mind, he couldn't get clear of the worry that *this time* his partner wasn't coming back.

And opening the body bag didn't help. Dante was *very dead*, his normally carefully styled red hair plastered to his gray-white face and closed eyes. Rick's hands trembled and his eyes blurred as he helped unzip the bag and attacked Dante's expensive suit with the scissors. He tried to keep the count down in his head and look at only the path of his scissors.

Director Leon swore. "Bullet went straight through." He looked at Rick, and at his shaking hands. "Pull it together, Rick. He's not going to care."

"You tell me to 'pull it together' one more time, I will punch you, regardless of the consequences." Rick snarled. He felt anxious and sick, his headache coming back with blinding fury. The pant legs were easy. The layers of sleeves, not so much. "How about you help unbutton his shirt or something useful."

Fortunately, the director complied without rebuking him for insubordination.

"Time's up, move." Director Leon grabbed Rick by his arm and pulled him to his feet as they both scattered outside the resurrection radius.

The job was far from complete, and Rick prayed that it was enough. He crouched on his heels and watched his partner's body intently, watching for the telltale smoke that indicated his partner was coming back to life.

The rest of the thirty seconds passed, and nothing. The fear that lingered in the back of his mind blossomed into panic. He wiped his hands on his nearly dry pants as even prayer failed him. He just stared numbly at his partner's body, not at all sure what he was going to do if Dante didn't resurrect.

Director Leon grabbed his arm and squeezed hard enough to bruise as he pointed at Dante's body. A faint wisp of smoke rose from

Dante's chest, and a sob caught in Rick's own. Rick raised his arm to shield his face as the smoke turned to a burst of searing flame. In a moment, the fire cleared to a smoldering ring of glassy sand with a very disoriented Dante standing in the middle.

Dante bent to pick up the one glove he'd resurrected with, then looked around, wariness and confusion on his face. The confusion became more pronounced and was laced with a fleeting look of fear when his eyes rested on Director Leon. He relaxed into visible relief when his scan stopped on Rick.

"Rick, man, where are my clothes?" Dante's look of consternation failed to mask the relief in his eyes. "Surely you had enough time to retrieve them by now. And my glove." He waved his bare hand. "I distinctly remember –"

Rick pushed his exhausted body to standing and fished the glove out of his pocket as the world tipped around him. He slapped Dante in the chest with the damp glove, cutting off his words.

"That's a start." Dante pulled the glove on with some difficulty, his eyes never leaving Rick. "*Mince*, you look terrible."

"It's good to see you, too." Rick snorted. He reached out and clasped one of Dante's gloved hands in his own, then pulled him in for a rough hug. He whispered huskily, "I'd almost given up hope."

Now that the danger was over and Dante was safe, the exhaustion, injury, and stress of the past day finally took their toll. Rick's shaky legs finally gave and he passed out against Dante's shoulder.

Chapter Twenty-Four

Dante awoke with a gasp and a sense of nauseated dizziness. He'd died, and taken longer than usual to resurrect, if the abnormal disorientation was any indicator. Anxiety edged into the disorientation as he scanned his surroundings looking for a clue to what had happened. And more than that, searching for his partner. A delayed resurrection meant his partner hadn't been able to get to him after he died. Why?

He saw only one glove on the ground in front of him and crouched to pick it up while he started to piece together his last few minutes before he'd died. The gunshot, Rick's injuries, fighting to stay alive until Rick woke up, the casket, beginning to fear Rick would not awaken in time – then Rick stirred. Dante looked at his bare hand. He'd given Rick his glove and tried to burn open the casket. Had it worked? If he was alive, that had to mean his partner had survived to rescue him. Right?

His eyes stopped on Charles and the confidence drained from his body. Unless someone reported seeing a casket go down and Charles himself had deduced it was him. Charles *had* been the one to pull him from Lake Michigan. Dante clenched his fists as his wary survey of the area became a frantic search for Rick.

There! Dante blew out a slow breath through his nose and tried to sound irritated, but not really caring that he failed at sounding anything other than immensely relieved, "Rick, man, where are my clothes? Surely you had enough time to retrieve them by now. And my glove." He waved his bare hand. "I distinctly remember –"

His partner pushed himself up on shaky legs and pulled the dirty glove out of his pocket. He slapped Dante in the chest with the glove.

"That's a start." Dante patiently wiggled his fingers into the sodden leather glove as he carefully scanned his partner for injuries. Blood, old and probably Dante's own, stained the same clothes Rick had been wearing when they'd faced Chick. His eyes were dilated and unfocused, probably from the blow to the head that had kept him unconscious in the casket. "*Mince*, you look terrible."

"It's good to see you, too." Rick snorted and clasped one of Dante's gloved hands – hands Dante hadn't failed to notice his friend carefully avoided in the past – then Rick pulled Dante in for an unsteady hug, leaned heavily against his shoulder, and whispered huskily, "I'd almost given up hope."

Rick's unsteady weight slumped against Dante as his partner passed out. Dante caught him with a cry and carefully carried him out of the still hot resurrection radius to lay him on the cooler sand beyond and get a better look at his injuries. He crouched beside him and gently examined his old stab wound and searched for a new head wound.

"Charles, why is he not in a hospital?" Dante kept his voice low and his eyes on his rapid assessment of Rick's condition, but his frustration with both his current partner and his former one was packed into his quiet question. Why could neither of them keep in mind that they were *mortal*?

"Tsk. You know any one of your partners past or present would rather die by your side than spend the night in safety while you're in danger." Charles must have seen Dante's alarmed expression, because he quickly sobered, "He refused to leave until you were safe. I've kept an eye on him the whole time. I'm pretty sure he's not going to die on us, but the ambulance is already on the way to make sure."

"You always think of everything, don't you, Charles." Dante's voice was still tight. Charles's strength as an agent, and more so as a director, was also his weakness: an uncanny ability to assess and utilize resources effectively, including human resources.

"I wasn't going to let him die, Dante. I need you both too much." Charles grunted. "But I also remember standing on a very similar boat in a very similar situation years ago. I wasn't going to cut him out as long as he wasn't a risk to himself or others."

Rick stirred and moaned as the wail of an ambulance siren sounded in the distance. Dante rested his hand on his friend's steadily rising and falling chest and watched his face grimly. "Get me my clothes, Charles. I want to ride with Rick to the hospital. I need to talk to Vikas again, without the council's interference, and I refuse to do it without making sure my partner is safe. Chick's not the only one who needs to answer for today."

RICK WOKE UP IN THE hospital *again*. For a groggy moment, he thought it was *still*. His side hurt so badly his mind immediately flashed back to the fight in the parking garage and the dollar store goblins with elf swords. Then he tried to sit up and his aching head brought back the rest of his memories.

"Easy." Dante's soft voice and gentle hand on his arm reminded him that his partner was alive and at his side again. "You took quite a beating the last couple days, no? After I apologized for keeping you from recuperating, I landed you back here again."

"It's better me here now than you at the bottom of the Potomac for the rest of time." Rick lay back and closed his eyes against the throbbing migraine.

"Yes. Charles said something similar." Dante sounded disgusted for a moment. Did the phoenix agent *resent* them putting their lives on the line for him?

"You've had human partners for *how long* and you haven't gotten it into your proud, pretty head that putting your life on the line for your partner is part of the job description?" Rick cracked an eye open and glared at him. It was incredibly unfair that his recently deceased partner was standing beside the hospital bed as infuriatingly suave as usual, while he was in it and barely able to tolerate the light enough to open his eyes.

"Perhaps. But usually I do a better job about not flagrantly disregarding their lives." Dante stood. "I intend to visit Vikas and make clear I will no longer tolerate this."

"Not by yourself you're not. He's already tried to kill you twice." Rick sat up fully and swung his legs over the edge of the bed, ignoring the nauseating way the room tipped when he moved. He reached for the IV line in his hand, but was stopped when Dante's gloved hand grabbed his wrist tightly.

"This is not Vikas. He's been an ally for over a hundred years. I helped him get elected to the council." Dante didn't seem interested in letting go of his arm, so Rick jerked it free. The baby-faced agent gave him a hard look, but continued without missing a beat, "I am convinced either Wharton or Laysha have his spirit ball. I have demanded an audience without their presence."

"I have no idea what any of that means, other than that you're planning to just offer yourself to him." Rick gritted his teeth against the nearly overwhelming urge to slap some sense into his partner. "You have a partner for a reason, keeping you alive being a big one. If you'd gone off to meet Chick alone, you'd probably still be at the bottom of the river."

Dante hesitated a moment as if Rick's words were getting past his fear and pride. "The person who possesses a kitsune's spirit ball can command the kitsune. If I can get Vikas without the others there, I might be able to figure out who's controlling him and help him get free."

"Or maybe he was already ordered to kill you on sight and you're dead no matter what, did you think of that?"

"Do you have a better solution? We've already seen that your presence isn't enough to stop them." Dante crossed his arms over his chest, but uncertainty lurked in the back of his eyes. "I will not *offer* you to him either."

"Get the director in here and we make a *real* plan, not some half baked cowboy scheme. If Vikas is playing enforcer for the warmonger factions, he knows who's behind the murders. This is PNI's case. Let's do this right."

"Charles will never agree–"

"And that should be your first clue that you're being an idiot." Rick closed his aching eyes and rubbed his eyelids. "Seriously, Dante, you're infuriating. You know that right?"

"Vikas needs to give account–"

"Once we have a plan, back up, and an escape route. We're not going back into what amounts to a mythic embassy without an extraction plan." Rick lay back against the pillows and closed his eyes. "Call Director Leon, then tell the nurse I need a painkiller and an exit strategy of my own. And, Dante?"

"Yes, *mon ami?*" Dante sounded tired and resigned as he gently pulled the blankets back up over Rick's shoulders.

"If you don't come back, Vikas will be the least of your worries."

IN THE END, DIRECTOR Leon refused to sign off on anything until Dante agreed to take Rick, set up the meet for a neutral location, and check in with a back up team on standby. Since Rick was going to be held in the hospital for another day, Dante had plenty of time to work out the details.

Rick was still wary that his partner was going to sneak off, or that facing Vikas was a fool's errand no matter what plans they made, but for the moment Dante seemed content to sit by his bedside and plan rather than running off half-cocked. He watched the red-headed younger – *older* – agent deftly place calls and send texts with grim determination. His watchfulness made it difficult to rest like the doctor advised.

"Rick, you must rest. If you are to be a player in this plot, I must have you as close to the top of your game as possible." Dante looked up from his phone and laid a hand on Rick's arm. "I give my word, I will not leave you behind."

"Did the director forbid it?" Rick yawned. He needed sleep. Not having to worry about his partner getting killed while he slept would help a lot.

"Quite emphatically." Dante chuckled. "And he is right. You both are. Being alone has never ended well for me. Please, just promise me that you will remember that I am immortal and you are not. If Vikas wants to try something, I will take the hit."

"Neither of us were going to survive the stuff he planned before, so I'm not agreeing to that. We both leave alive, Dante. That's the plan." Rick rolled over with his back to his partner and wiggled deeper into the covers to rest. He trusted Dante to be as good as his word.

Rick drifted in and out of sleep, always awakening to find Dante there, attentive to his needs. He wasn't sure when or if the phoenix slept, but when he finally awoke to the shift change the next morning, Dante was pacing the room and ready to leave. He spoke to the nurse briefly about getting a doctor in to clear Rick for discharge, then pulled his chair closer to Rick's bedside and sat down, looking at his partner intently.

"I have arranged the meeting for Shamus Finnegan's office after hours. Vikas seemed reluctant, but agreed to all the conditions. I told him this was the last stop before PNI brings him in for questioning officially." Dante shrugged. "He has no choice."

"Shamus didn't really strike me as a neutral third party." Rick frowned as he carefully tried to sit up again. Dante reached out and laid a hand on his back to support him, a concerned look on his face. The dizziness passed quickly, so he dangled his legs over the side tentatively.

"No one is truly neutral." Dante looked at Rick skeptically and didn't remove his hand. "Finnegan spoke up for me, yes, but he is on the council, and he made no move to defy Vikas after the verdict. The bank is secure, and we will be alone. It is also filled with cameras if Vikas decides to betray us." He paused and offered his arm when Rick tried to rise from the bed on shaky legs. "You do not have to do this. Charles can find someone else."

"You forget Vikas and his warhounds tried to kill me as well." Rick leaned on his partner heavily before finally getting steadier and waving him off. "Three times, if we're keeping count. I am going. At this point you can't stop me." He looked down at his hospital gown and frowned, then looked his partner square in the eyes. "My clothes, man. Surely you don't think I'm going out like this."

Dante snorted a very undignified laugh. "Ah, I'm afraid I am unprepared. Forgive me. I cannot even offer you my spare set."

"I'd go out in my hospital gown first." Rick grumbled, then sat down hard on the bed.

"I can go home and get you something." At Rick's skeptical look, Dante added hastily. "I promise I will return before the meeting, if you promise to rest while I am gone."

"Deal. Easily." A couple more hours couldn't hurt.

Dusk found them knocking at the door of the closed bank. The Leprechaun co-owner quickly opened the door for them, then locked it again behind them.

"Vikas is in the conference room waiting." Finnegan scrambled to keep up with Dante's long, determined stride. "Remember what you promised. No fire. I won't have you burning my conference table like you did at the Council building."

"You will not have to worry about that if Vikas doesn't try to *kill* us." Rick grumbled. His head still hurt, and his patience with *all* mythics, including his partner, was wearing thin.

"He has promised to cooperate and tell you whatever you want to know." Finnegan opened the door to the conference room and gestured for them to enter. He pulled the heavy hardwood door closed with some effort and locked it behind them.

Vikas sat at the table, his hands folded in front of him, but his back ramrod straight and his eyes wary. He didn't look particularly cooperative to Rick.

"Dante. Agent McCoy." Vikas nodded to them but didn't rise. They didn't sit either.

This was going *so well* already.

"Vikas. We have been allies for longer than you have been president of the mythic council. I believe you owe me some answers." Dante's voice was calm and even, maybe even a little soothing. "Someone has your spirit ball, don't they."

"Yes." Vikas answer was more an angry snarl than an actual word. His hands in front of him hardened into fists. "I cannot tell you how sorry I am for what they have made me do – may still make me do."

"Did they make you look the other way while they killed people and tried to incite the humans and mythics to war?" Dante's tone didn't change, but he put a gloved hand on the edge of the heavy table and leaned against it toward the kitsune. "Nothing happens in the mythic world without your knowledge."

"You know that they did."

"Did they make you kill Ms. Moore to frame me?"

"I would need a lawyer before I answered that, Dante."

"So, yes?" Rick offered, earning him a glare from the kitsune.

"Who is it, *camarade*? My partner and I will find him and free you." Dante took a step back from the table and started to round it toward the mythic leader. "You know you can trust me. Is it Wharton? Laysha?"

Rage simmered in the kitsune's eyes and his gaze darted behind Dante.

Before Dante could turn, he stopped with a sharp intake of breath and froze. Rick turned quickly to see what startled his partner and saw Shamus Finnegan with a knife to his friend's back.

ALEXANDRA GILCHRIST

Chapter Twenty-Five

Dante felt something prick against his back just above his belt. He arched his back away, but could still feel what seemed to be a sharp knife digging into his spine. "Et tu, Shamus?"

"When the mythic council failed to remove the threat you made to my plans, I'd hoped you and your partner would at least get the hint and stay out of our business." The leprechaun dug the knife in deep enough to cause a droplet of blood to trickle down his spine beneath his shirt. "Do you know who benefits from war, Brand? Bankers. Governments need money fast, so they take out loans. An urban war like this means rapid money movement on every government level, not just the national one. When bankers thrive, so do the leprechauns."

"You killed all those people?" Rick gave Finnegan a skeptical look even while he kept his hands in the air. "I know you didn't attack me. Those guys were taller. And uglier."

"There is no shortage of mythics willing to 'throw off the chains of human oppression' or even just cause mayhem, especially if the price is right." Finnegan scoffed. "I just keep an eye on things to make sure it goes as planned."

"Was Faircloth in on it?" Dante reached subtly for his glove, only to get a jab to the back hard enough to make him cry out.

"Lay off, Lucky Charms," Rick warned in a gravelly tone. "I have a gun, and you only have a knife. If you hurt my partner I will end you faster than you can clean the blade."

"Faircloth was a rube. He trusted me fully and didn't ask questions." Finnegan pointed his free hand at Rick's holstered gun. "And I'm going to need you to slide that to me before I sever Agent

Brand's spinal cord and leave him a cripple. I'm not stupid. I know what happens if I kill him. I don't have any intention of doing that yet."

Rick gave Finnegan a hate filled glare as he carefully lifted the handgun from its holster with two fingers, laid it on the floor, and slid it toward the leprechaun.

"Good. Vikas, take the human." Finnegan put his foot on the gun and gestured to Rick.

Vikas rounded the table and pinned Rick's arms behind his back with little struggle from the other agent, who kept a concerned eye on the knife at Dante's back.

"You have his spirit ball," Dante realized. "That's why he's obeying you. He has no choice."

"It took me decades to get my hands on it." Finnegan pulled a glowing gold ball out of his pocket and held it in his hand. "I rule the council now, and with you two out of the way, a civil war between humans and mythics will be assured."

Dante laughed softly. "I do not envy you when Vikas gets free. Kitsunes hate being controlled. And Vikas will be especially vindictive because you forced him to do something against his principles."

"I do not intend for him to get free." Finnegan stuffed the ball back inside his pocket, grabbed Dante's belt with his free hand, and twisted the leather tightly enough the buckle bit into Dante's stomach. "Just like I don't intend for you to be able to stop me." He pulled back on the belt and leaned in, pushing the knife deep into Dante's spine.

Dante screamed in pain, even as his legs buckled and he dropped to the ground like a rag doll. He landed hard on his left forearm and hip, screaming again as he snapped a bone in his arm. He felt nothing below the knife, which Finnegan didn't even bother to remove. He heard Rick calling his name somewhere beyond the fear and pain.

"He's still alive, but I'm afraid he's no use to anyone anymore." Finnegan kicked him in the ribs out of spite, and the lack of pain threatened to tip Dante into a panic attack.

"I believe in God, the Father almighty..." Dante began to pray the Rosary under his breath, even though there was no way to reach it in his pocket. It steadied him and cleared his mind as he rolled onto his stomach, tucked his broken arm against his chest, and propped himself up on his right arm.

"Vikas, kill them both. I don't care how and I don't want to know. Just make sure Dante doesn't come back." Finnegan turned for the door as Vikas took Rick by the neck.

"If you kill him, I will burn anyone that comes within arm's reach of me. I will use whatever power remains to me to burn this building to the ground." Dante pulled the glove off his uninjured hand with his teeth and spat the glove back to the floor. "And when you kill me to stop me, I will come back and wreak vengeance on you both and every leprechaun and kitsune in the entire city."

Both Finnegan and Vikas froze.

"Let him go and I will submit to whatever Vikas has planned." *Holy God, help me.* Dante ran a dry tongue over lips parched with fear. "My infinite lives for his one. Surely a mere human can be no threat to your plans."

"Don't be stupid, Dante–" Rick cried out, but was quickly silenced by Vikas tightening his grip on Rick's throat, prompting Rick to grab his hand with both his own to pull it away enough to allow him to breathe.

"Wharton was right. You have sold yourself to the humans." Finnegan gave him a derisive look. "How do I know that you will keep your word?"

"I have always kept my word." Dante met Rick's angry glare with an apologetic look of his own. "It is as we discussed, no? When one of us has to die, it must be me."

"You know this isn't what we discussed at all, you stubborn phoenix," Rick rasped past Vikas's chokehold.

"I'm not a fool. He's a human cop, and will name me as soon as he's free." Finnegan waved a careless hand. "Burn the city down for all I care. It will give the humans more to blame on the mythics. All the same, I intend for Vikas to make sure that's impossible." He passed the gun to Vikas. "If either of them resist, kill the human first. Burn him so the cops who find him think Dante did it. Burn him alive if it keeps Dante in check. I don't care. Just take care of them. I'm going to take care of the Vice President. When the human ally of the dragon king drowns on dry land, civil war will be inevitable."

As soon as Finnegan walked out of the council chamber and closed the door behind him, Vikas threw Rick aside in disgust.

"Holy God, have mercy." Dante rested his weary head on his forearm. The prospect of dying – even permanently – didn't seem quite as onerous as watching another partner die. He lifted his head and looked at Vikas. "Vikas please, can you not fight him? You know this is wrong."

"You heard him, both of you. Just because he's not here, doesn't mean I don't have to obey." Anger battled with pity in Vikas' eyes. "But he did say I can do it my way, so I will try to be as merciful as possible. None of that dark magic garbage Laysha and Wharton tried to pull."

"Thanks, I guess." Rick rolled his eyes as he pushed himself to his feet and made his way to Dante's side. "If I'm going to die, I'm so glad I'm not going to have my body desecrated after. When I'm dead. And don't care."

"Kindly shut up, Rick," Dante whispered. He pushed himself up on his elbow and glared at his partner. "I would rather not tempt him to repeat that."

"Don't worry. Wharton and Laysha didn't need to be that elaborate. Deep water would have been enough. Finnegan has a wall aquarium in his office. Once I mercifully euthanize you both, I can place Dante's body in there to keep him from resurrecting until such a time as the Council thinks best to allow him to do so."

"Hear that, Dante, we're calling murder 'merciful euthanization' now." Rick scoffed.

"You may call it whatever you like, but realize it is inevitable." Vikas turned for the door as well. "I suggest that you make your peace with God and each other while I prepare the aquarium. If either of you cause trouble while I'm gone, I will be forced to make your deaths less comfortable."

"Sit Rep, partner." Rick sobered as soon as Vikas was out of hearing. "You went down hard and haven't moved, so I'm guessing it's bad."

"I have no feeling below the knife, which hurts like hellfire every time I move. I have a broken ulna and quite possibly a rib where Finnegan kicked me. I cannot tell, because I cannot feel my ribs there."

"I can pull the knife free, if that will help." Rick sounded less than confident, but followed through with ease.

Dante gasped, then nearly sobbed in relief that the blade was gone.

"What else can I do?" Rick pulled off his shirt and used it as a pressure pad to stop the bleeding. "I'm not really interested in finding out what Vikas thinks is 'merciful euthanasia.'"

"I can't say I am either, but you will not like my suggestion." Dante rested his head again, more this time to avoid looking at his partner's face when he said the unavoidable.

"You're going to have to kill me."

Chapter Twenty-Six

"Not happening." Fear grabbed Rick by the throat with more force than Vikas had.

"If you do not, we will both die, somewhat more permanently." Dante's voice was soft, nearly muffled by his face buried in his arm. He didn't look up, but he sounded perfectly calm, perfectly resigned, as if he'd asked Rick to drive home because he was tired or something. "You can't face Vikas on your own, and I am worthless this way."

"Don't you think I understand that?" Rick realized he was shouting and forced his words through tightly clenched teeth. "I can't kill someone in cold blood, much less my own partner. There has to be another way." He looked at the slowly growing dark patch on Dante's back, not growing nearly fast enough to cause him to bleed out on his own.

Dante finally raised his head and looked at him with pain and fear. "I am open to suggestions, but we are running out of time before Vikas comes back."

Rick stared down at the knife still in his hands, trying to think of any other solution that would not require him to murder his own partner, but now that the suggestion was made, all he could think about was the different ways he could use it to end Dante's life most effectively. He dropped the knife with a clatter between them.

"If it makes you feel any better, Vikas left the knife knowing full well what you could do with it. He doesn't want to do this, but his hands are tied. If we're still here when he returns, he will have to complete the orders given to him."

"It does *not* make me feel better, thank you very much." Rick scowled at his partner. "Can't you do it yourself? Surely the Church won't hold it against you if you resurrect anyway."

"No, it won't, and as much as I loathe it, I have done so in the past." Dante nodded to his broken arm with a grimace of pain. "But I doubt I can do so efficiently with only a dagger and one hand. I cannot even roll over to free that one hand without your aid."

"Do you realize what a terrible thing you're asking me to do?" Tears began to burn in Rick's eyes.

"I do. You know that I do." Dante shuddered under Rick's hand. "I was in your position not too long ago. And I hope that at the resurrection, Wes can forgive me. But I will resurrect much sooner and *you* do not have to die today. I beg you, please, do not hesitate any longer."

Rick knew Dante was right, and he hated him for it. Unreasoning anger welled up in the place of the fear. Anger at his partner for placing this responsibility on him, himself for what he was about to do, and – God forgive him – anger at God himself for leaving them no other option. *God, why does it have to be this way?*

Trust in the Lord with all thine heart; and lean not unto thine own understanding. A familiar verse prodded his heart.

I don't understand, Lord, and I certainly don't like it. Rick gritted his teeth and screwed his eyes shut against the tears that burned his eyes. *But I choose to trust You anyway.*

"What do I need to do?" Rick couldn't keep the anger and disgust from his voice, and he didn't care. Nature itself rebelled against every detail of this plan.

"Help me roll over." Dante's apologetic voice took a hard edge of determination. The immortal knew what this was doing to him, but persisted anyway. Trusting God's plan in this meant trusting his infuriating partner as well.

Rolling Dante over *gently* without coming in contact with his deadly bare hand was impossible, and Rick winced when Dante cried out in pain as his broken arm was jostled.

Rick sat back on his heels and listened with growing horror as Dante gave him clinically detailed instructions about the fastest and most reliable technique to slit his throat. He tucked his hands under his legs to hide how much they shook and clenched his teeth against the nausea roiling in his stomach.

Dante gave him a sympathetic frown. "You may find it easier if you cover my face."

Ahh, nope. Rick glanced at the exit, knowing full well there was no way to get through the thick, locked wood door without Dante's fire. Dante's suggestion that he cover his partner's face to give him distance from what he was doing made him nearly panicked enough to try anyway. He was trapped in his worst nightmare.

A noise in the hall snapped him back to reality. They were out of time and there was only one escape.

"If we both survive this, I'm calling in that steak dinner." Rick made a grim attempt at a joke as he reached a shaking hand for the knife he'd dropped.

"If we both survive this, I'll buy you the biggest steak dinner you have ever eaten." Dante chuckled softly. "Godspeed." He closed his eyes and relaxed, tilting his head up and away to expose his throat.

Rick almost threw up then, at the sight of his friend baring his neck to him in total trust. What kind of world required friends to kill each other? He swallowed hard, took the bloodied shirt he'd used as a bandage, unfolded it, and laid it across Dante's face. He laid on hand on Dante's shoulder and braced himself.

Dear God, forgive me. He pressed the blade exactly where Dante had instructed, squeezed his eyes closed, and followed through.

It was harder than it looked on TV, and Dante's blood burned on his hands and bare chest – whether from guilt or the fire that brought him back to life Rick didn't know. And he didn't care. He leaned over and vomited until he couldn't vomit any more, then crawled out of the resurrection radius, curled into a ball, and wept.

"DO YOU REALIZE WHAT a terrible thing you're asking me to do?"

"I do. You know that I do." Dante shuddered at the memory of having to take Wes's life. *Holy God, why have you not spared him this grief?* "I was in your position not too long ago. And I hope that at the resurrection, Wes can forgive me. But I will resurrect much sooner and *you* do not have to die today. I beg you, please, do not hesitate any longer."

Dante tried to think of a way he could take the burden from his partner, and if Rick still refused, he might have to. He was done arguing, surely Vikas couldn't delay his return much longer. By all that was holy, he'd lean on the blade himself if it spared him the loss of Rick. He'd have done so already if he'd had any confidence in his success.

"What do I need to do?" The anger and disgust in Rick's voice worried him a little, but if it meant they lived, Dante supposed he could accept his partner's abhorrence. It would be a steep price, but one he could stomach if they walked away.

"Help me roll over." Dante cried out in pain as his broken arm was jostled, but he didn't dare brace it with his other while his hand was still bare. His own fire couldn't kill him, but setting his suit on fire would make Rick's task much more difficult.

Rick's face went from pale to ash gray edged with green as Dante gave him explicit instructions about the fastest and most reliable technique. "You may find it easier if you cover my face."

His partner almost backed out then, he saw it in the panicked way Rick flinched away from him. *God, give him strength.*

A noise in the hall snapped Rick back to reality with a start. The panic faded from his face and a muscle tightened in his jaw.

"If we both survive this, I'm calling in that steak dinner." Rick reached a shaking hand for the knife he'd dropped.

"If we both survive this, I'll buy you the biggest steak dinner you have ever eaten." Dante chuckled softly. "Godspeed." He squeezed his eyes closed, forced himself to relax, tilted his head up and away to expose his throat. Even though this had to be done, it was still going to be unpleasant. Even as an immortal who had died more times than he could count, his God-given conscience rebelled over just lying there and allowing someone to take his life. *God be merciful to us both.*

He felt the soft, blood dampened cloth cover his face, and clenched his free hand against the revulsion that shuddered through him. Rick needed him to remain calm, to not show his own fear and disgust. Rick's trembling hand gripped his shoulder, and Dante calmed his ragged breathing to keep from projecting his own dread to his partner.

He caught his breath as the sharp edge of the blade pressed to his throat. A nagging voice of panic told him to fight, that he needed to *live.* The pain in his arm and lack of all feeling below that demanded otherwise. Their *lives* demanded otherwise.

Rick leaned against him and the blade bit deeper. Dante tensed against the searing pain, then relaxed as his lifeblood drained, and quickly passed out.

Dante woke again with a gasp. He looked around the conference room in confusion, struggling to remember how he *died* here, desperate to eliminate any threat to him and his partner.

Rick. His memory of his last few moments started to clarify and he scanned the room for his friend. There, curled in a corner by the wall sat Rick with his back to him.

"Rick?" Dante bent to pick up his gloves and pull them on. When his friend didn't answer, fear tripped his heart. Surely he hadn't been harmed in the resurrection blast. Vikas would soon claim his whole attention, but he needed to make sure Rick was all right first.

He crossed to his partner's side, and crouched to lay a gloved hand on Rick's bare back, which was blistered from burns and rose and fell in ragged breaths. "Rick, I–"

"If you say one word to me about what just happened, I swear the next two words out of my mouth will be 'I quit,'" Rick snapped without turning around.

Unhurt then, at least physically. Dante sat back on his heels and nodded. He hesitated a moment and blew a slow breath through his nose. "I need to deal with Vikas. You get out of here and take the back up team to stop Finnegan and get Vikas's ball." He hated the idea of sending Rick into danger, but more lives were at stake than just his partner's or his own. *He's proven himself a more than capable agent.*

"Ha. Not a chance." Rick barked a sharp laugh. "You're the most helpless immortal I've ever met. You need me. What if you die again?"

"Well, I cannot destroy any more clothes. Not like this." Dante gestured to his embarrassingly bare chest.

Rick snorted as he pushed up to standing. "It wasn't good enough to burn up your own clothes, you had to go and burn *my* shirt too?" He grimaced as he dabbed the blood from his face and hands with a nearby curtain. "How bad is it?" Blistered burns covered his face, hands, and chest wherever Dante's blood had touched at his resurrection.

Dante winced. "It will heal. I am sorry."

"Don't." Rick raised a hand to stop him as the door opened to admit Vikas. "Just get us out of here and we'll call it even."

"I will get *you* out of here and occupy Vikas. Once you have his spirit ball, *everyone* will be out of danger, including me." Dante lay a gentle hand on his partner's shoulder. "I'm trusting you not to get yourself killed, please do not make me regret this."

"Give me an opening." Rick sighed his resignation. He slid over to the wall beside the door, waiting for Vikas to open it. "Just try not to let me find you floating in the fishtank when I get back."

Dante nodded grimly, clenching his teeth to hold back the reminder that him floating in the aquarium was very far from the worst case scenario here. "God be with you, *mon ami.*"

The door swung open to reveal Vikas, fire in his own hand.

"Vikas!" Dante pulled free both his gloves and dropped them to the floor without taking his eyes off the kitsune. He needed to draw the fox shifter inside before he realized Rick was standing by the door. He lit a flame in his left hand while he gestured to their opponent. "I do not want to kill you, just as I know you do not truly want to kill us."

"What I want is irrelevant, Dante. It's only what I've been *ordered* that matters." Vikas matched his pose. His gaze flicked to Rick and indecision crossed his face.

Mince. He needed Rick out of this room before fireballs started flying. "Were you ordered *not* to return Agent McCoy's gun to him?"

The corner of Vikas's mouth twitched. "I was not." He pulled the pistol from his waistband, and handed it to him. "But I *was* ordered not to let him leave, so it will do him no good."

"So we win by finding loopholes?" Rick whispered as he snatched his gun from the kitsune, darted out of his reach, and checked the magazine.

"It is the only way you win against a mythic. I thought everyone knew that." Dante chuckled. So far Vikas hadn't made an aggressive move toward his partner, but the moment Rick tried to leave that would change. He needed to make an unignorable distraction, and an alternate route of escape for Rick. Humans could survive a leap from a second-story window. He'd seen many of his partners walk off from one. He moved quickly to the window to his left and laid his hand on the frame, melting out the glass. "Your orders were to not let us escape, but you're going to have to make a choice, Vikas. When you face

Finnegan again, which of us do you want to report is free, and which do you want to report is dead?"

Rick gave him an uneasy look, as if uncertain if Dante was sending him away so he could sacrifice himself.

Vikas in turn gave Rick an uneasy look, as if still uncertain if he could kill the human agent before facing the immortal one.

Dante didn't give him a chance to decide, he dove toward the kitsune in a high tackle, grabbing him and knocking him out of the door into the hall as his shirt burst into flames. Vikas retaliated by punching Dante twice in the nose. Neither of them could be harmed by fire, so they grappled with fists, knees, elbows, and feet as weapons instead. Vikas was an inferior fighter, but Dante wasn't trying to win. He was only trying to keep the Mythic leader busy until Rick could retrieve his spirit ball. In the meantime, this would be the longest stalemate in his life.

Holy God, speed him on his way.

Chapter Twenty-Seven

As soon as Dante took the kitsune out the door, Rick went out the window, tucking and rolling as he hit the narrow strip of grass outside. The agents watching as back up spotted him fast and a heavily armed agent scrambled to his side and escorted him to the perimeter.

"Agent Brand?" The agent – Agent Milton, if Rick remembered correctly – glanced back toward the window expectantly.

"Not coming." Rick ground his teeth, suddenly aware it looked like he'd abandoned his partner. The agent's momentarily horrified look prompted him to add, "He's buying us time. We need to stop the little Irishman that left here about half an hour ago. He's going to try to kill the Vice President."

"Finnegan?" Another agent, one with unnaturally sharp teeth that made Rick suppress a shudder, came up beside the first. "The *banker*?"

"Apparently warmongering is a lucrative side hustle. He hurt Dante, so don't let his size fool you." Rick looked the man over. If he was going to use this team to take Finnegan down, he needed to understand his assets. "No offense, agent, but I need to know, what are you?"

The man glanced at his partner nervously. "Werewolf, sir. We're not all aligned with Wharton."

"Good to know." Rick briefly wondered if the Mythic Council fracturing would ripple out into PNI, then decided that if he, Dante, and the Vice President were going to survive that day, those questions would have to wait. He looked at the human agent he first encountered when he went out the window. "Hand me your phone, I need to call the director." He held out his hand expectantly. He may have been with PNI for only a couple months, but he still out ranked these men.

The man fished it out, tapped in the lock code, and offered it to him without objection. "You're sure we can't help Dante? We've got a werewolf, a giant, a dryad, and three fully armed human agents. Vikas wouldn't stand a chance."

"Vikas is being controlled by Finnegan. Some spirit ball thing. I assume you know what that means because Dante didn't have time to explain, and I really don't have time to wait for explanations. Dante would rather not kill the kitsune for something he can't control, but Vikas won't stop hunting Dante until we stop Finnegan." Rick dialed the number he now had recognized and put the phone to his ear to wait for it to ring. "Mobilize your team. We need to move as soon as I'm done here."

The man nodded and the pair of agents jogged off to obey.

"Hello?" Director Leon answered warily.

"Rick McCoy, Director, we have a bit of a situation."

"Welcome to life as Dante's partner. What do I need to know?"

"Shamus Finnegan is our man. He has Vikas's spirit ball and is using him to incite a human mythic civil war for financial gain. He's on his way to murder the Vice President and pin it on the mythics." That was an awful lot of words Rick wouldn't have imagined himself using a couple months ago, much less using confidently. "Dante is keeping Vikas occupied and I'm taking the back up team to intercept Finnegan. Can you alert the Vice President's protection detail?"

"I'll handle it. Do we know which mythic guild he plans to frame?"

"Only that whoever he planned to frame was a water type." Were they Pokemon now? Rick stifled a laugh. The thought of his partner as a fire type Pokemon was never going to leave his head.

"Makes sense. Vice President Lee is attending an aircraft carrier dedication this afternoon. The carrier's named after his grandfather. I'll make sure the agents working security there know to accommodate your team and look out for Finnegan. Godspeed, Agent McCoy."

So they were his team now. Alright. He'd been a team leader in New York. Not a team like *this*, but he'd use it to his advantage. He handed the silent phone back to the agent returning with his team. He looked over the small group swiftly. Six agents, four male and two female, one of each definitely over six feet tall. Director Leon had chosen this team for brute strength, but hopeful Rick could get some speed from them as well. They looked at them expectantly, waiting for his lead.

"There's a plot on the Vice President of the United States. Shamus Finnegan, king of the Leprechauns, has Vikas's spirit ball and is preparing a water attack on the VP at the Navy Yard." He scanned their faces to make sure they were following. They seemed to be. "The VP's team has been alerted. Our job is to intercept Finnegan if possible and retrieve Vikas's spirit ball. Any questions?"

The agent's looked at each other and shook their heads.

"Good, I guess. I'm going to need your names and what guilds you belong to." Rick rubbed the bridge of his nose. "We're going to catch a leprechaun."

DANTE HAD DIED ONCE already. Vikas had gotten his hands on Finnegan's knife before he could and had used it very effectively. Fortunately, getting his body to the aquarium had turned out to be a bigger task than the kitsune expected and Dante had resurrected in the doorway of Finnegan's office, torching the heavy desk, rich carpet, expensive wallpaper, and Vikas himself. Vikas was uninjured, but the intensity of Dante's resurrection fire destroyed his clothes and drove him back long enough for Dante to gather his wits. Served him right. Served him and the faithless leprechaun right. The overhead sprinkler system had activated, dousing them both and eliminating any further risk of them burning the bank down.

"Your human will fail. Finnegan is too strong." Vikas dove on him before he could fully recover and knocked him back over the desk chair to the charred carpet below. "Pietro didn't stand a chance against him."

The implication that Vikas's human partner had been killed by Finnegan himself stunned Dante long enough for Vikas to take another jab at him with the knife he still held. Dante tried to roll out of the way, but Vikas had him pinned and the blade scored several ribs. He hissed out a pained breath, flung Vikas off him, and scrambled to his feet. He clutched his hand to his bloodied side, circled out of Vikas's reach, and asked breathlessly, "Is that how he got your spirit ball?" *Keep him talking. Keep him busy.*

"Pietro protected my spirit ball with his life, but it wasn't enough. Your human will lose his life retrieving it and it still won't be enough." Vikas leaned back and brandished the knife.

Ice threaded Dante's veins. "Rick is a highly trained agent."

"Pietro was a former Marine. It didn't matter."

"Rick is aware Finnegan is a threat. He won't be caught off guard."

"Is he aware of what a leprechaun can do? Does he know he can teleport?"

Dante froze again. He had no idea *what* Rick knew about leprechauns, but based on his previous reactions to other mythics, he guessed it to be next to nothing. His uncertainty cost him again. Vikas came at him with the knife again and this time he didn't react in time. It caught him low, entering just above his hip bone and tearing out his side as he twisted away. He stumbled and fell to one knee, the room tipping as blood slicked his hip and leg. Whether he planned to kill Vikas or not, he was going to have to get that knife away from him before he died to it a third time. If Vikas got free to chase after Rick, his partner *would* be in grave danger.

"Rick will adapt. He has before. He took out three of Wharton's dogs and held three others at bay while he arrested Wharton himself." Dante found himself panting, the knife had to go and the aquarium had to be destroyed. Probably the aquarium first, because the knife had done its damage already, and if he wanted to be alive in a few minutes instead of literally floating with the fishes, the aquarium had to be out of the equation.

But if he destroyed the aquarium, would Vikas fall back to his original plan to corrupt his heart to keep him from rising? Rick was out of the way and there were no other innocents for him to use, but that didn't mean there wasn't another way.

"You seem to think your partner is invincible." Vikas sneered. He had the upper hand, and he knew it. "Once you are dead, he will be too."

"Whether you succeed in killing me or not, I have faith in my partner's abilities." Dante forced himself up on shaky legs and backed toward the wall aquarium. "And I have more faith still in the ability of our God to protect him without my help."

A small tell, and Dante knew Vikas was about to charge him. He smiled wearily. Vikas could have waited for his current injuries to take their toll, but he chose a foolish offensive move instead. Dante pressed one hand against the glass to melt a hole in it, grabbed the knife blade in his bare hand and melted it to a rivulet of searing steel running down his arm, then leveraged Vikas over his shoulder into the compromised aquarium glass. Vikas's weight punched a large hole in the safety glass, knocking Dante off his feet in a deluge of water, glass shards, and floppy fish. Dante rolled to his side, pushed himself to his knees, and shook off the water as best he could. Even the movement made his awareness flicker. He'd managed to take out the aquarium in time. Being *wet* wasn't the issue, being *submerged* was, and by Vikas colorful cursing behind him, the kitsune knew it as well.

"Foolish *bird*." Vikas sloshed through the soggy carpet toward him. Rage threaded his voice. He cursed Dante's origin creatively. "I tried to have mercy on you within the parameters of the commands I am bound to. Now you have forced my hand. You will resurrect this time, but I promise you it will be your last."

Dante clenched his teeth as his shaky limbs gave out and deposited him in the soggy plush carpet. *I have faith in my partner and my God. Your threats mean nothing to me.*

Chapter Twenty-Eight

Rick flashed his badge to the guard at the gate of the shipyard, who nodded them through as if he was expecting them. Director Leon said that he'd make some calls, so they probably were.

"Finnegan never gets his hands dirty, but he heavily implied he watched all the murders from a distance." Rick addressed the men in the SUV with him. Agent Milton was driving, since the PNI issue car was signed out to him and he was apparently familiar with the shipyard. "So we need a place he can observe without being spotted coming too and from."

"Well leprechauns can teleport, so, that's basically anywhere with a view." Agent Milton scoffed. One of the guys in the back had a disdainful look, like he couldn't imagine how such an obvious noob like Rick could have a higher rank than him.

"Oh, joy. So that means as soon as he realizes something is off, he's gone." Rick rubbed the bridge of his nose. He didn't know the first thing about leprechauns or any of this . He *was* a terrible noob. *Lord, help my inexperience not cause the mythic war of the millenia.* "How long do we have before he starts to suspect he's compromised?"

"The VP isn't supposed to arrive for another twenty minutes, and is notorious for being late. So, thirty maybe." Agent Milton parked the car and shrugged.

"We split up then. Teams of two – one mythic, one human. You spot him, you fall back to report to me and stand down until I get there." Rick twisted in his seat to look back at the rest of the team behind him. "Vikas promised not to stop until Dante is *dead*-dead, and Finnegan won't stop until a bloody human-mythic war is assured.

Catching him and getting Vikas's spirit ball is the only way to stop them both."

"You realize that catching a leprechaun used to be a really big deal, a nearly impossible task." Agent Milton glanced sideways at him. "So much so that people expected a pot of gold if they did it."

"I'd be satisfied with a kitsune spirit ball and my partner's life, thanks." Rick scanned the shipyard and the crowds gathering at a dock harboring a massive ship. "Can he teleport in the murderer?"

The team shook their heads in unanimous uncertainty. Delightful.

"All right. Here's the plan. I see three possible locations. There, there, and there." Rick pointed out the windshield at some tactical observation points. One he wasn't sure how a team could get to *without* teleporting. "The VP's team can take care of protecting him. We'll focus on stopping Finnegan so he can't kill again."

Lord, give us your grace to succeed and give Dante the strength to hold out until we do.

The three teams split up and headed into different directions. Agent Milton left his phone with Rick so they could contact him, and Rick waited in the car so he could back up whichever team found Finnegan. No offense to Director Leon's hand picked backup team, but he wasn't sure he trusted any of these men with Dante's life, much less the power to control a powerful immortal and avert a civil war. Once someone spotted the rogue leprechaun, Rick would move in to close the deal. Maybe these psychos could get the point that *his* partner was off limits as well.

In the meantime, waiting was terrible. His mind replayed the last moments he'd spent with Dante – Finnegan's attack, his partner paralyzed and helpless, and what he'd had to do to save him – in *very* vivid detail. And he'd allowed Dante to persuade him to leave him behind to face a kitsune bent on his destruction alone. By the time the cell phone rang, his hands were trembling at the memories.

He cleared his throat twice before he managed to answer firmly, "Agent McCoy. Do you see him?"

"We do. He's standing on the flight deck of the new *USS Enterprise* in dry dock watching the proceedings." The voice on the other end of the phone paused. "You'll never get to him without spooking him."

"Let me worry about that. Just don't let him see you." Rick hung up and stared at the partially constructed aircraft carrier. Various cranes and scaffolding surrounded the vessel, so getting up itself wasn't necessarily impossible. Getting up without being seen by a suspicious supervillain with a bird's eye view was. He needed help. He dialed the director again.

"Agent McCoy, do you ever use your own phone?" Director Leon asked the moment he answered.

"Well, apparently these nuts you send me after think destroying my phone is a sporting event. At this rate, PNI is going to have to budget cell phone replacements into my expense allowance like you do Dante's suits."

"Who told you we–"

"Unless you're paying him way more than you're paying me, there's no way he's replacing all those fancy suits himself." Rick laughed at the director's slip up. "That's obviously not why I called. I need a distraction in about fifteen minutes. Nothing serious. Just something that will hold Finnegan's attention while I sneak up on him."

"I can manage it. And just so you know, the Vice President is out of danger. Take that jerk down."

"I intend to." Rick hung up, called in the other two teams as back up, stuffed the phone in his pocket, and slipped out of the SUV.

"I'm going up after him by myself." Rick told the leader of the team waiting on him as soon as they rendezvoused. "But I need you right behind me in case it goes south. I'm not facing a ticked off leprechaun without backup."

The pair nodded, the agent with the disdainful face looking at him doubtfully, but silently.

Rick sat on the edge of the scaffolding nearest the point they had indicated Finnegan waited, slipped off his shoes, and handed Agent Milton's phone to the skeptical agent. He didn't need anything that might give him away. Then he started climbing, counting down to when the director's distraction would take effect and praying it didn't scare his opponent away.

He reached the top and cautiously peered over the rail at the little red-headed man sitting on the front edge of the flight deck, his legs dangling over. There was probably the length of a football field between them. He'd have to be swift and silent to grab the treacherous leprechaun before he vanished.

The crowd grew silent, and Finnegan leaned forward as if watching something intently. Director Leon's distraction? Loud music, like the cross between a marching band and a rock concert, rose up from the docks. Finnegan seemed captivated, so Rick made his move.

He pulled himself up onto the flight deck, then dashed toward Finnegan, his socks cushioning his footsteps and the music covering any other noise he might have made. Halfway there. The leprechaun was enthralled by the music, his legs swinging in time to the beat. Three quarters. The leprechaun stiffened as if suddenly aware something was wrong. Rick dove, praying he didn't take both of them off the side. The leprechaun could teleport to safety, and he'd be a smear on the bottom of the dry dock.

Finnegan's face registered surprise just as Rick closed his hand on the leprechaun's arm and skidded to a stop at the edge of the flight deck.

"So you captured me. Lucky you. By rights you've earned my treasure." The leprechaun's eyes were bitter and cold as Rick dragged him away from the edge.

"The only treasure I want from you is Dante's life and Vikas's freedom." Rick panted to catch his breath as he squeezed the leprechaun's arm tighter. "Give me the spirit ball."

Finnegan hesitated, then eyed the edge of the flight deck as if considering pitching either the spirit ball or Rick himself over the edge. Rick pinned the leprechaun to the flight deck, remembering Dante's words about loopholes as his back up team clambered over the rail onto the deck.

"That's how it works, doesn't it? As long as I don't let go, you can't disappear and you're obligated to give me the treasure. You know what I want." Rick thrust his free hand into Finnegan's pockets as he dug for the ball. His hand closed on it and he pulled it free. "Bingo."

He kept his hand closed tightly around Finnegan's arm as he sat back on his heels and stared at the ball. This was the key to everything, but he had no idea how to use it.

"Just say his name." The disdainful agent suggested, less contemptuously than Rick expected.

"Vikas, I summon thee." Rick spoke to the ball, ignoring the eye rolls from the three men watching him. "Hey, you guys aren't being super helpful here, so if I have to be left with what I learned about mythics from movies, that's on you."

The other two agents had the decency to look embarrassed as Vikas appeared out of nowhere, his expression startled and his hands bloodied. He also appeared to only have one tail remaining. He took one look at the spirit ball in Rick's hands and his eyes narrowed angrily.

"You can teleport. Good." Rick lifted the ball and his captive. "These are yours. I want my partner in return."

Vikas hesitated, and for a moment Rick feared it was because there was nothing left of Dante for him to retrieve. Then, in a blink, the kitsune was gone. Rick held his breath. Dante had been left with the vengeful kitsune for a long time. More than enough time for the kitsune to activate whatever his creative backup plan was to "mercifully euthanize" his partner.

Another blink and they both appeared. Vikas shoved Dante forward and the agent stumbled to his knees in front of Rick. Rick tossed the ball to Vikas and released Finnegan without a second look at either of them as he knelt in front of his partner and lifted his chin so he could get a better look at his injuries. Blood, bruises, and cuts mottled his body, one arm was clutched awkwardly to his chest, and a matted lock of red hair fell over one swollen black eye, but a relieved grin met Rick's concerned gaze.

"Looks like I owe you that steak dinner."

Chapter Twenty-Nine

The Brazilian Steakhouse was *expensive*. Rick could tell that just by walking in. The subtle lighting, the elegant chandeliers, the cut flower arrangements, and the immaculately set tables gave an ambiance of sophistication that was far beyond the family dining chains Rick was more used to. The director had made the reservations, and PNI was paying, so Rick was determined to enjoy himself and not ask too many questions. The waitress took him to a table with a white tablecloth set for three and took his drink order. The director already sat there, poking at his cell phone.

"Director Leon." Rick greeted him as he pulled out a black, wooden chair and sat beside the older man.

"Charles, please." Director Leon laid his phone face down on the table and looked at Rick. "Dante's partners form a rather exclusive club. You'll come to appreciate what I mean in time."

"I'm beginning to already." Rick pushed the memory of their time in the bank away before it got going. "Where is our illustrious partner?"

"Probably just getting out of the shower." Charles scoffed as he stood to go to the buffet. "It's a wonder we weren't late to every assignment. I guess after several centuries, he's well aware of how long he takes."

"I live with him, remember." Rick stood to follow him. "It was literally his alibi when he faced the mythic council, remember? I nagged him to get out of the bathroom several times the morning Ms. Moore was killed."

"That saved his butt once in the seventies." Charles filled his plate with vegetables as he spoke. "His powder blue bell-bottomed suit was lost at the cleaners in Vegas and one of my predecessors had to make an emergency run with him to confront the cleaner. Their hotel room was blown up while they were gone. It was well into my tenure before he stopped using it as proof that it pays to take care of your appearance."

They had just returned to their table when the waiter approached with Dante in tow. Dante approached the table with a heavier step than he usually had. It was clear by his stiff movements and tight expression that the man was still in pain. He wore a burgundy three piece with white lapels and cuffs. His right arm was in a black sling, and he hissed out a low breath when he accidentally bumped his side against the edge of the table as he lowered himself into the chair across from Rick.

"Are you wearing *makeup*?" Rick narrowed his eyes as his partner and pointed at him with his fork. "You *are*." He nearly choked on suppressed laughter. "You really are a *peacock*."

Dante touched his swollen eye gingerly with one gloved finger. The fingertip came back with a light tint of concealer. "If you had looked like I did this morning, you'd wear makeup as well."

"No chance. Not until I'm dead." Rick snorted. "And only because I don't want the guests at my funeral to think I'm a zombie."

"Zombies look better than the face that greeted me in the mirror this morning." Dante grumbled, focusing his attention on the medium well steak in front of him.

"Hey, you should just be glad you're still alive." Rick paused to direct the waiter to serve him a cut of well done brisket.

"Hmm. You're sure I can't get you to reconsider that?" Dante wrestled with the steak with his left hand for a moment before sighing in frustration.

Charles reached for Dante's plate, but Rick beat him to it without thinking. Dante began to protest, but only earned himself a dirty look from both his companions.

"You have better odds of getting me to put on makeup." Rick gestured at his partner with the steak knife and started cutting Dante's steak for him. "Also. Not talking about that. Ever again. Not unless the next thing you want to do is star in your own reality show where you torment potential partners as you whittle your way down to the poor sap who has to put up with you."

"Isn't that what I did with you?" Dante gave him an infuriatingly saccharine smile.

"Look in a mirror, pal. I'm not the one who looks like he's been through the gauntlet." Rick laughed as he started cutting the steak in smaller pieces. "Newsflash. A broken arm, two broken ribs, and a messed up face *aren't* terminal injuries."

"You are as stubborn as a *bulldog*." Dante snarled and snatched his plate back from Rick. A few stray pieces of meat tumbled into his lap at his rough movement.

"Lucky for you." Charles interjected, the big grin on his face showing he was enjoying their banter. "Rick's stubbornness is the only reason you're not at the bottom of the Potomac, or buried who knows where by Vikas."

"Granted. And I am grateful. Bulldogs can be loyal and protective as well as stubborn." Dante sobered as he stabbed at his meal awkwardly. "Rick also stopped Finnegan before he could kill again. Without my help, and in direct defiance of his previous skepticism."

"It's kinda hard to remain a skeptic after everything we've been through in the last month." Rick washed down a bite of potatoes with his Coke. "Whatever happened to Finnegan anyway? Vikas didn't eat him, did he?"

Dante made a choked squawk and hastily took a long drink of Cabernet to avoid inhaling his dinner by laughing.

"No, of course not." Charles chuckled. "Finnegan is in mythic custody and relatively unharmed, all things considered. It's up to the DA to decide whether to allow the mythics to try him or sue for extradition."

"After our experience with Mythic' 'justice', I'd recommend extradition." Rick swallowed with a grimace. "Unless you'd really like someone to eat him – or worse."

"Now that Vikas has his spirit ball back, PNI has no concerns in that area." Charles shrugged dismissively, then paused as the waiter came by with another long skewer of meat, this time with a rack of ribs on it. After directing the waiter to place some on his plate, he continued, "For now, the threat of a Mythic war has been averted."

"Not bad for our first case." Rick smiled at Dante. "Though, if we're going to continue this partnership, we're going to have to take you to an outlet mall. Find you some clothes people *actually* wear this century." Rick picked up Dante's left arm by the embroidered hem of his suit coat between a thumb and forefinger and made an exaggerated grimace. "Peacock."

"You're stuck with me. You wouldn't have it any other way and you know it." Dante gave a soft, musical laugh. "Bulldog."

Dante was right, of course, but Rick wasn't about to admit that out loud. Rick shook his head as he stood to take another trip to the buffet. He waited until he was just behind Dante's line of sight and messed up his partner's perfectly styled hair.

Dante let out an indignant squawk that turned to a low hiss when he turned too fast and hit his arm on the table.

"Peacock." Rick repeated softly. A month ago, he'd stood in Charles's office and scoffed at everything about Dante Brand. Now he couldn't imagine another man by his side. Dante was right, he wouldn't have it any other way.

Don't miss out!

Visit the website below and you can sign up to receive emails whenever Alexandra Gilchrist publishes a new book. There's no charge and no obligation.

https://books2read.com/r/B-A-YYCV-ZJZKC

BOOKS 2 READ

Connecting independent readers to independent writers.

Also by Alexandra Gilchrist

A Rick and Dante Paranormal Mystery
Baptism by Fire

Standalone
Song of the Stars

About the Author

Alexandra Gilchrist has loved stories of great adventure, deep friendships, and noble ideals since she learned to read. Realizing it was becoming more and more difficult to find those kinds of stories in today's culture, she decided her only recourse was to write her own.

When she's not writing (or wishing the stories were done so she could just READ the blasted things), she enjoys spending time with her husband and kids, deep diving theology at 11pm, watching anime, and cuddling her cat.

Milton Keynes UK
Ingram Content Group UK Ltd.
UKHW040729030823
426269UK00001B/70

9 798223 551744